SPELLBOUND

POWELL HAYLLAR SADLER

ONE

M

Copyright © C. J. Powell, R. K. Sadler, T. A. S. Hayllar 1978

First published 1978 by
THE MACMILLAN COMPANY OF AUSTRALIA PTY LTD
107 Moray Street, South Melbourne 3205
6 George Place, Artarmon 2064
Reprinted 1978, 1980

Associated companies in
London and Basingstoke, England
New York Dublin Johannesburg Delhi

National Library of Australia
Cataloguing in publication data

Powell, Clifford J.
  Spellbound one.

  Index.
  ISBN 0 333 25134 2.

  1. Spellers. I. Hayllar, Thomas Albert S.,
  joint author. II. Sadler, Rex Kevin, joint author.
  III. Title.

428'.1

Set in Century by Modgraphic, Adelaide
Printed in Hong Kong

Contents

Acknowledgements

Cartoon art by Marilyn Newland

The authors are grateful to the following for permission to reproduce the photographs.

The Health Commission of New South Wales (p. 2); the Veterinary Division of Bayer Australia Ltd (p. 19); Leyland Motor Corporation of Australia Ltd (p. 21); John Fairfax & Sons Ltd (pp. 27, 121); Woolworths Limited (pp. 32, 74); The *Manly Daily* (p. 36); Uncle Ben's of Australia Pty Ltd (p. 41); Qantas Airways (p. 45); Mullins, Clarke and Ralph (Vic) Pty Ltd for BHP, illustrator Bruce Weatherhead (p. 53); NSW Permanent Building Society (p. 69); Australian Institute of Pertroleum Ltd (p. 80); Grace Bros Pty Limited (p. 86); Stafford-Ellinson Suits (p. 90); Medibank (pp. 95, 107); Western Plains Zoo (p. 98); Mount Cook Airlines (p. 112); Dunlop Footwear (p. 115); Lufthansa German Airlines (p. 124)

Preface

Good spelling is no accident. It has to be worked on. The recognition of the one and only grouping of letters that goes to make up a word is no easy skill to acquire. Ideally, words should be taken apart, put back together, looked at in a variety of ways and, above all, *used*. But nobody said this has to be boring!

In the authors' view, there's real learning value in making spelling a pleasure, not a task. *Spellbound One* (written specially for lower and middle secondary students) presents over 600 everyday words in 30 categories. None of the words is given a chance to lie idly about in lists. They all find themselves pushed around. In puzzles, games and exercises they are dismantled, reconstructed and generally made to work hard. So do the students! But, that's life. Words won't work for you unless you *use* them.

As the key to real motivation is both need and interest, *Spellbound One*

- puts 600 vitally useful words into the student's and teacher's hands,
- provides ways and means of coming to grips with these words so that interest is kept up and the spell of gaining control over word construction is unbroken.

Well, as spelling is all bound up with words— good spellbinding!

1 **MOVEMENT**

ARRIVE	FOLLOW
APPEAR	RETURN
ADVANCE	LEAVE
APPROACH	CARRY
HURRY	RAISE
HAPPEN	REMAIN
ACTIVITY	REACH
ENERGY	PERFORM
REMOVE	STRUGGLE
COMING	ESCAPE

1 Which one will you use?

Other forms of some of the words from the spelling list are bracketed after the sentences below. Write out the sentences, putting in the correct form of the word from the brackets as you go.

(a) A burst of cheering greeted each new .... as he or she stepped from the plane. [arrive, arriving, arrival, arrived]

(b) You need to be fit and full of .... to do well in the .... sport of canoeing. [energy, energize, energetic, energetically]

(c) Surfers take a really .... interest in their strenuous .... [activate, actively, active, activity]

(d) Some people say that in water-skiing either everything goes smoothly and nothing much .... or everything begins .... at once! [happen, happens, happening, happened]

(e) Several big circuses run three or four .... a day and feature .... horses. [perform, performed, performs, performances, performing]

2 Add and Arrange

(a) Add these words to your spelling list: DIVE, WALK, SPRINT, ACT, LUNGE, SWIM, PLUNGE, HASTEN, CLIMB, DANCE.

(b) Arrange all thirty list words alphabetically.

3 Opposites (called Antonyms)

Here are four groups of letters (called prefixes) that will give opposite meanings when added to the front of certain words.

DIS   UN   IN   UN

Use each one to turn these words into their opposites.

(a) activity	(b) appear
(c) approachable	(d) hurried

4 Words with similar meanings (called Synonyms)

To complete the word chain you need 12 words from the spelling list. The clues are all words with similar meanings to the words you have to find.

1.
2.
3.
4.
5.
6.
7.
8.
9.
10.
11.
12.

CLUES
1. lift
2. fight
3. power
4. replace
5. gain
6. haste
7. stay
8. advance
9. transport
10. shift
11. act
12. reach

5 More Opposites

Line up each of the words on the left with its opposite on the right:

(a) coming   arrive
(b) raise   replace
(c) leave   depart
(d) remove   going
(e) arrive   lower

6 Box words

Two words are mixed in each of the boxes below.
However, the first letter of one word and the last
letter of the other are circled. Work out the words.
All ten words are from the spelling list.

(R) e e m o
　　　 m i a e v r (N)

(A) i d r a v
　　　 c n r v a e (E)

(A) i c r t v t
　　　 i a i s y (E)

(E) s t e g r
　　　 a u g p s l c (E)

(H) e h p r
　　　 u n p a r (Y)

7 Grids

You can have a lot of fun with this one. Make a
copy of the grid below. Then fill in the squares with
examples of items starting with the letters in the
spelling word along the top. The first square is
filled in to show you how.

	R	E	A	C	H
Feelings	Rage				
Girls' names					
Boys' names					
Foods					
Animals					

8 The big A

Below are some would-be words sharing A — the big A. Find the words — they are all words from your list.

2 Thinking

BELIEVE	DOUBT
DECIDE	REASON
CHOOSE	MEMORY
IMAGINE	CERTAIN
GUESS	INTELLIGENT
SUGGEST	WORRY
THOUGHT	DISAGREE
IDEA	FORGET
OPINION	UNDERSTAND
SUPPOSE	CONSIDER
REALIZE	AGREEABLE
ANSWER	EXPECT
KNOW	

1   Double letters

Fill in the missing letters.

(a) Choose

(b) Intelligent

(c) Agreeable

(d) Guess

(e) Suppose

(f) Suggest

(g) Disagree

(h) Worry

2 Noun making

Change these words into nouns.

(a) believe	(b) realize
(c) understand	(d) know
(e) expect	(f) decide
(g) suggest	(h) certain

3 Crossword

Copy this crossword into your workbook. All the words are in the spelling list.

CLUES
1. Positive
2. Look forward to
3. Think about
4. Select
5. Understand clearly
6. Think out
7. Clever
8. A plan of action ✓

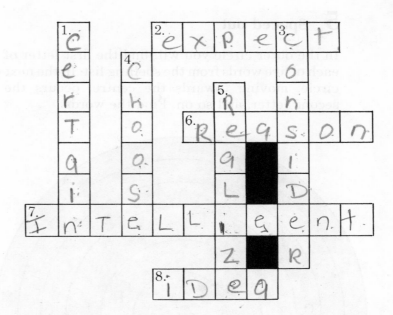

4 Opposites

Add prefixes to the following words to form their opposites.

(a) certain	(b) understand
(c) intelligent	(d) believe
(e) agree	(f) decided

5 Spaced out

In the outer circle you will find the first letter of each of five words from the spelling list. In the next circle, moving towards the centre, occurs the second letter, and so on. Find the words.

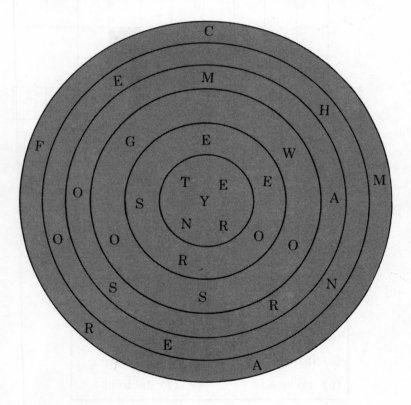

6 Blanks

Use these words to complete the sentences.

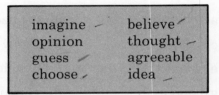

imagine	believe
opinion	thought
guess	agreeable
choose	idea

(a) Do you *believe* in God?

(b) In my *school* our headmaster is a good administrator.

(c) Since the weather was pleasant, the family *thought* it would be a good *idea* to go to the beach.

(d) My mother can never *choose* between two dresses.

(e) It is not good enough to *guess* the answer to a question.

(f) Can you *imagine* what life would be like on a desert island?

(g) We were all *agreeable* to going to the pictures when the picnic was cancelled.

7 Expansion

(a) decide — dec_o_c_ion

(b) imagine — imag_i_n_a_t_i_o_n

(c) know — knowl_e_dg_e_

(d) doubt — doubtf_u_l

(e) intelligent — intelligen_c_e

(f) reason — reason_e_bl_e_

(g) memory — memor_e_bl_e_

(h) consider — consider_a_tion

(i) expect — expect_a_t_i_o_n

(j) suggest — suggest_i_o_n

8 Mixup

Unscramble the letters to form list words.

(a) w o n k

(b) g é n j i a m

(c) n ó s e a r ✓

(d) e i o d c s r n

(e) i i p n n o o

(f) m ÿ r e o m

9 A useful spelling rule

The sound 'eee' is often represented in words by 'ie' and 'ei' (e.g. belief and deceive). There is a very good rule to help students. It goes as follows. When you have the sound 'eee', use 'i' before 'e' except after 'c'. After 'c' you use 'e' before your 'i'.

Now fill in the blanks for the following 'eee' sounds.

(a) bel_ie_ve   (b) rel_ea_ve

(c) dec_ei_ve   (d) gr_ee_f

(e) th_ea_f   (f) ch_ea_f

(g) rec_ei_ve   (h) c_i_ling

(i) y_ee_ld   (j) sh_ea_ld

QUARREL	DISCUSS
REFUSE	APOLOGY
QUESTION	PROMISE
MENTION	ADVISE
INFORM	EXCLAIM
DECLARE	ANNOUNCE
ARGUE	ADMIT
EXPLAIN	ORDER
LISTEN	STUTTER
PRAISE	REQUEST

3 Speaking

1 Lineup

Write down the words from the first column below. Then select the correct meanings from the second column.

✓	(a) quarrel	assurance that no offence was meant ✓
✓	(b) listen	allow entrance to
✓	(c) apology	argument between people ✓
	(d) request	glorify or commend
	(e) admit	ask for
✓	(f) praise	hear a person speaking with attention

2 Roundabout

Complete the circular puzzle. The last letter of each word is the same as the first letter of the following word.

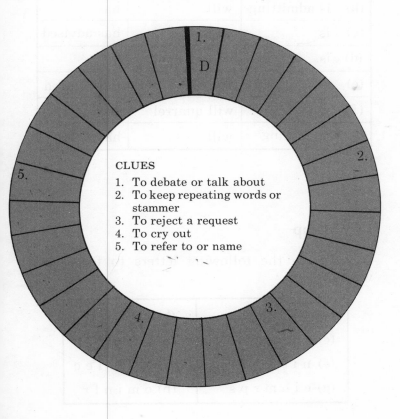

CLUES

1. To debate or talk about
2. To keep repeating words or stammer
3. To reject a request
4. To cry out
5. To refer to or name

3 Noun making

Write the nouns from the following verbs.

(a) refuse	(b) inform
(c) argue	(d) declare
(e) explain	(f) discuss
(g) exclaim	(h) announce
(i) admit	

4 Missing

Fill in the missing letters.

(a) _ _ _ _ r r _ _	(b) _ e _ _ _ _ _ n
(c) _ r _ _ s _	(d) _ e _ _ e _ _
(e) _ _ o _ o _ _	(f) _ n n _ _ _ _ _
(g) _ _ _ _ _ s s	(h) _ x _ _ _ _ n

5 In go the blanks

Insert the following words in the appropriate blank spaces.

admit ✓	apologized ✓
listened	announce ✓
explained ✓	promised
advised ✓	arguments ✓

People had been .... to arrive at the concert early. Each ticket said '............ one.' The compere was forced to .... that the star had been delayed and there followed many .... among the crowd. When the performer finally arrived he .... that he had been delayed at the airport. He .... to his fans and .... to sing a number of extra songs for them. The crowd .... intently and agreed that the concert had been a great success.

6 Tenses

Complete the following table.

(a)	is	will announce	has
(b)	is admitting	will	has
(c)	is	will	has advised
(d)	is	will apologize	has
(e)	is	will	has refused
(f)	is	will quarrel	has
(g)	is arguing	will	has

7 Mixup

Unscramble the following letters to form list words.

(a) n n i t o m e	(b) r e d o r
(c) t t t u s e r	(d) v i a d e s
(e) n i s e o u t q	(f) d e a r l e c
(g) e i o m r p s	(h) o m i n f r

COMPLETE   CONSTRUCT

FINISH   DAMAGE

BEGINNING   PREPARE

ATTEMPT   MANAGE

REPAIR   METHOD

ACHIEVE   COMMENCE

BUILD   CONTINUE

USEFUL   SKILFUL

CONNECT   SUCCEED

ORGANIZE   ACCURATE

4 DOING, MAKING, CREATING, COMPLETING

1 Completing

Using the correct form of the word in brackets, complete the following sentences.

(a) I have no further .U........ for my old briefcase. [useful]

(b) The sign on the shop said, 'Under new ....' [manage]

(c) The film will be .... at 8 o'clock. [commence]

(d) The violinist played .... [skilful]

(e) Have you .... your homework yet? [beginning]

(f) The .... for the school play took many months. [prepare]

2 Changing parts

Complete the table.

	NOUN	VERB	ADJECTIVE
(a)		commence	
(b)	damage		
(c)		complete	
(d)		build	
(e)		organize	
(f)	method		
(g)		continue	
(h)		succeed	

TOOLS

3 Code

Every second letter of the following 'words' will form a list word. From each 'word' form two list words.

(a) s a k c i h l i f e u v l e

(b) m m a e n t a h g o e d

(c) a c t o t n e n m e p c t t

(d) r f e i p n a i i s r h

(e) c b o e n g s i t n r n u i c n t g

(f) a c c o c n u t r i a n t u e e

4 Nouns

Write down the nouns from the following words.

(a) connect		(b) construct	
(c) useful		(d) achieve	
(e) accurate		(f) skilful	
(g) manage		(h) prepare	

5 Crossword

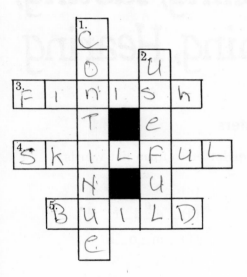

CLUES
1. to keep up
2. of use
3. to end
4. clever
5. to construct or make

6 Opposites

Add one of the prefixes 'in', 'un', or 'dis' to the following words to form their opposites.

(a) continue	(b) prepared
(c) complete	(d) skilful
(e) connect	(f) accurate
(g) repair	(h) finished

7 Mixup

Unscramble the following letters to form words from your list.

(a) shinfi	(b) efuuls
(c) nicotune	(d) cuseced
(e) zionrage	(f) hiveace
(g) tttmpae	(h) ripear

5 Smelling, Tasting, Touching, Hearing

SCENT	SMOOTH
PERFUME	ROUGH
TONGUE	MOIST
BITTER	SQUEEZE
TASTE	TOUCH
SOUR	MOUTH
SWEET	SCREAM
APPETITE	ALOUD
FRAGRANT	DEAFEN
DEODORANT	SILENT

1 Missing letters

Fill in every other letter to form list words.

(a) _p_e_i_e   (b) _o_s_

(c) _e_f_n   (d) _e_d_r_n_

(e) _i_e_t   (f) _m_o_h

(g) _e_f_m_   (h) _o_g_e

2 Sensory words

Humans have five senses (sight, hearing, smell, taste and touch). Find a list word associated with each of these senses.

(a) hearing	(b) touch
(c) smelling	(d) taste

3 Code

From the table we will code the letter 'a' as A1, the letter 'r' as D4, etc. Use your table to decode the following words from your list.

	A	B	C	D	E
1	a	b	h	n	t
2	e	c	j	p	v
3	i	d	k	q	w
4	o	f	l	r	x
5	u	g	m	s	y

(a) B4, D4, A1, B5, D4, A1, D1, E1.

(b) D5, B2, D4, A2, A1, C5

(c) E1, A4, A5, B2, C1

(d) B1, A3, E1, E1, A2, D4

(e) D5, A4, A5, D4

(f) A1, C4, A4, A5, B3

(g) D5, B2, A2, D1, E1

(h) C5, A4, A5, E1, C1

4 Crossword

CLUES

1. Sweet smell
2. Even or polished
3. One of the five senses (connected with the mouth)
4. Agreeable odour
5. Organ in the mouth concerned with tasting
6. Deprive of hearing
7. Part of the face used for eating

5 Noun making

Write the nouns from the following words.

(a) rough	(b) fragrant
(c) deafen	(d) silent
(e) moist	(f) bitter

6 Spaced out

Fill in the spaces with list words. The first or last letter has been given.

(a) A lemon has a b............ ....e.

(b) The ....e of some flowers is very strong at night.

(c) The baby's s............ upset his mother.

(d) The grass was ....t with dew and it was easy to slip on its s............ surface.

(e) Very loud music can ....n people.

(f) S............ and s............ chicken is a popular Chinese food.

7 End up

Write down the list on the left-hand side of your page. Then add the correct ending to each word from the right-hand column.

(a) per	st	(e) appet	nt
(b) bitt	ite	(f) tong	ent
(c) moi	fume	(g) deaf	er
(d) sil	ue	(h) sce	en

BREEZE	HUMIDITY
THUNDER	VISIBILITY
LIGHTNING	DIRECTION
HURRICANE	FORCE
SHOWER	SOUTHERLY
CLOUD	OVERCAST
STORMY	TEMPERATURE
WEATHER	OCCASIONAL
REPORT	FLOODING
FORECAST	GALE

6 The Weather

1 This one's a breeze

Use the meanings in brackets to help you find the words that fit the sentences.

(a) The announcer read out the .... and then gave the district .... [the degree of heat; an estimate of future weather]

(b) The .... was poor and the sky was .... [the distance that can be seen; grey and cloudy]

(c) The wind was a .... and before long it reached .... force. [a wind from the south; strong wind]

(d) The weather was .... with .... claps of .... and flashes of .... [unsettled; happening from time to time; the sound of the storm; electrical display]

(e) In the tropics where the .... is usually high, any .... makes a big difference to comfort. [the moisture or dampness in the air; light movement of air]

2 You and U

Given the U's from six words in the spelling list, find the words.

```
_ _ _ u _

_ u _ _ _ _ _ _ _

_ _ u _ _ _ _ _ _

_ _ _ _ _ _ _ _ u _ _

_ _ u _ _ _ _

_ u _ _ _ _ _
```

3 Fumbled forecast

The weather turned out to be just the opposite to that expected from the forecast. Write out the forecast, changing each word in italics to its opposite. (The opposites are all list words.)

Tomorrow's forecast is for *clear* skies, *fine* days, but *continuous* showers at night. *Drought* is expected in the west. Winds should be *northerly*.

4 Weather words

Weather words have been divided into four groups and the words in each group can be fitted into the crossword. To start you off, one word in each crossword has been fitted in. See if you can fit in the others.

(a) *Wind words:* breeze hurricane direction force gale southerly

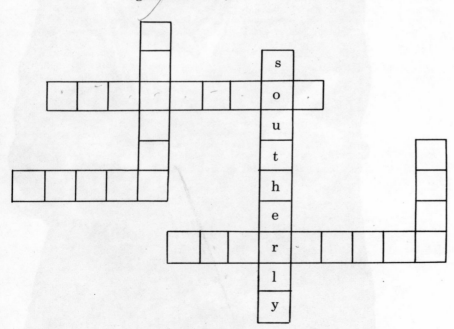

(b) *Water words:* humidity flooding shower cloud

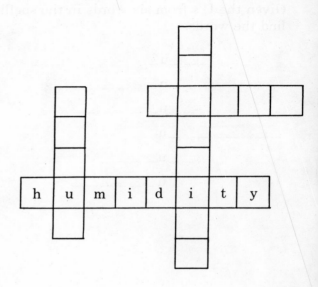

(c) *Light and sound words:* lightning visibility thunder

(d) *Weather bureau—all-purpose words:* stormy weather report forecast overcast temperature occasional

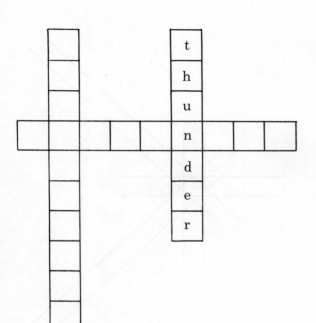

5 Shares

Four words from the list share an 'o' and four share
a 'c' in the diagrams below. Work out the words.
(Arrows show where the words begin.)

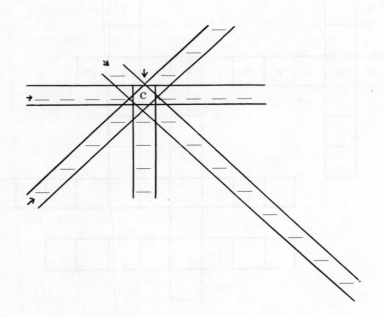
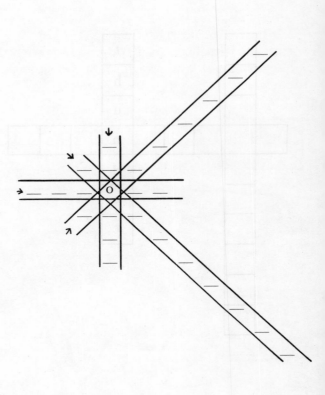

6 Words within words

VISIBILITY and OCCASIONAL are two words from the list that contain other words within them. See how many other words you can squeeze out of each one.

	words squeezed out
VISIBILITY	
OCCASIONAL	

7 Getting back together

To the left and right are strange-looking groups of letters. Look more closely and you will see that they are really words from the list that have been forcibly separated. The first, third, fifth, seventh, ninth, etc., letters of the list words have been placed on the left. All the leftover letters have been placed on the right. *Your job:* Get the words back together. One has been put back together as an example.

t u d r ⟶	thunder ⟵	h n e
h m d t	_____	u i i y
t m e a u e	_____	e p r t r
l t g i g	_____	i h n n
d r c i n	_____	i e t o
s u h r y	_____	o t e l
f r e	_____	o c
s o e	_____	h w r
o e c s	_____	v r a t
f r c s	_____	o e a t

7 SURFSIDE

COSTUME	BOARD
TOWEL	UMBRELLA
SURFER	SURFACE
CURRENT	DEPTH
WARMTH	SHORE
RESCUE	SWIMMING
PATROL	CAUGHT
DROWN	PLEASURE
DANGER	ENJOYMENT
WATER	SUMMER

1 Blanks

Insert the following words in the appropriate blank spaces.

costume	shore
surfers	towels
summer	danger
current	rescued
umbrella	

One .... day we decided to go to the sea .... to swim. We packed our .... and .... , making sure not to forget the beach .... to protect us from the sun. There was a large sign which read '............ , swim between the flags.' A strong .... had dragged a number of .... out into deep water and lifesavers had .... them.

2 Change over

Change the subject of the following sentences as shown.

(a) The lifesaver rescued the swimmer.
The swimmer ....

(b) The swimming season begins in October.
The beginning ....

(c) Diving into shallow water can cause spinal injuries.
Spinal injuries ....

(d) Fishing can be a very relaxing pastime for many people.
Many people ....

3 Syllables

Rule up the following table in your workbook. In the first column write all the list words with one syllable, in the second column all words with two syllables and in the third column those words with three syllables.

One syllable words	Two syllable words	Three syllable words

4 Snake

Fill in words from your list.

5 Code

a	b	c	d	e	f	g	h	i	j	k	l	m	n	o	p	q	r	s	t	u	v	w	x	y	z
n	o	p	q	r	s	t	u	v	w	x	y	z	a	b	c	d	e	f	g	h	i	j	k	l	m

Each letter in the top row will be coded by using the letter underneath it (e.g. k=x, s=f). Decode the following list words.

(a) j n e z g u   (b) c y r n f h e r

(c) q r c g u   (d) c n g e b y

(e) r a w b l z r a g   (f) f u b e r

(g) p b f g h z r   (h) h z o e r y y n

6 Verbalize

Write the verbs from the following words.

(a) warmth   (b) enjoyment

(c) surfer   (d) swimming

(e) pleasure   (f) depth

7 Shuffle

Unscramble the following sentences.

(a) Our swimming enjoy pool in we.

(b) The sharks patrol of beach warns.

(c) Glass as the pool as the surface was smooth of.

(d) Very baby in drown a shallow can water.

MANAGER	SHELVES
BARGAIN	TROLLEY
SPECIAL	CASHIER
PACKAGE	GROCERIES
VALUE	WRAPPED
STORE	BASKET
REGISTER	FROZEN
PRICE	ADVERTISE
BOUGHT	WEIGHT
AFFORD	PIECE

8 At the Supermarket

1 Select the correct form

In the blank spaces in each sentence, use the right form of the word in brackets at the end of the sentence.

(a) Beef and lamb .... are expected to rise in the next few days. [price]

(b) A price freeze will not be successful as far as .... items are concerned. [groceries]

(c) The goods are being .... in the refrigerator. [store]

(d) The supermarket is .... its new range of chocolates. [advertise]

(e) Butchers are always .... their meat. [wrapped]

(f) Tender .... of chicken are available. [piece]

(g) The customer was .... fresh vegetables. [bought]

(h) The piece of ham .... 250 grams. [weight]

2 Mixed-up meanings

In the first column are words from your list. Write them down. Then next to them write down their correct meanings from the other list.

(a) store   reasonably cheap

(b) manager   person in charge of money

(c) afford   unusual or exceptional

(d) value   money for which a thing is bought or sold

(e) special   a person conducting a business

(f) cashier   to have enough

(g) price   worth

(h) bargain   stock

3 The rule for adding '-ing'

When words end in 'e', drop the 'e' before adding 'ing'. Examples: smile — smiling; shave — shaving. Now try adding 'ing' to the following list words.

(a) package	(b) value
(c) price	(d) store
(e) piece	(f) freeze

4 Make up words from your list

Write down the first column. Then add an ending from the other column to form a word from your spelling list.

(a) val	gain	(e) bask	ier
(b) man	ped	(f) reg	age
(c) pack	ister	(g) cash	et
(d) wrap	ager	(h) bar	ue

5 Filling in the blanks

Fill in the blanks and complete the words below.

(a) _ _ n _ _ e _

(b) _ _ o _ e _ _ e _

(c) _ e _ g _ _

(d) _ _ el _ _ _ _

(e) _ a _ _ _ i _

(f) _ a _ _ e

(g) _ o _ _ h _

6 Completing sentences

Use these ten words to complete the sentences.
Each word can be used only once.

bought	afford
manager	store
wrapped	register
groceries	value

(a) The .... instructed his staff at the supermarket to .... the fruit in the warehouse.

(b) The customer could not .... to buy all the
.... in her trolley.

(c) The butcher .... the meat which the customer had ....

(d) A new cash .... had arrived.

(e) The package was real .... to the customer.

7 Magic rectangle

The letters of *three* words from your list have been
scattered through the rectangle. What are the
words?

s	o	p	i	f	i
n	z	l	p	r	e
a	c	e	e	c	e

8 Word jumbles

Write down the word from the list for each of the
following.

(a) e a c p g k a

(b) l a c i p e s

(c) n a r a b i g

(d) i r e t e s g r

(e) i c r a h e s

(f) h e w i g t

(g) t o g u b h

(h) f a r o d f

9 *Your Sporting Life*

COMPETITOR	OPENING
UMPIRE	SELECTED
SCORE	SPECTATOR
BOUNCE	PENALTY
APPLAUSE	COACH
GOAL	SERVE
SEASON	OVAL
ACCURATE	ABILITY
CAUGHT	WHISTLE
PASS	FOUL

1 Mixed meanings

Line up words and meanings correctly.

(a) spectator   clapping and cheering

(b) umpire   chosen to play

(c) penalty   spring up after striking the ground

(d) applause   skill and knowledge

(e) accurate   a sports ground

(f) ability   a disadvantage given for breaking a rule in a game

(g) selected   exact

(h) bounce   a person who decides disputes

(i) whistle   someone who looks on at a sport

(j) oval   a little object that gives a shrill sound when blown

2 Same sound — different spelling — different meaning

Some words sound the same but are spelt differently and have different meanings. Don't confuse them! Here are two words from the list together with possible confusions.

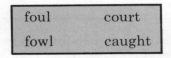

foul	court
fowl	caught

Now, see if you can slot them correctly into the following sentences.

(a) The captain was .... out after making a century.

(b) A netting fence protected the .... yard.

(c) The referee signalled a ....

(d) The game was played on a grass ....

3 Specs

The Latin word *spectare* means 'to look at'. Our word *spectator* comes from the Latin word and means 'someone who looks on at a sport' rather than actively taking part in it. The following unfinished words also come from the Latin word *spectare*. Their meanings have been given to help you work them out.

(a) spec _ _ _ _ _ _   used to assist eyesight

(b) i _ spec _ _ _ r   a person who looks closely at things

(c) spec _ _ _ _ _   a great display

(d) spec _ _ _ _ _ _ _ _   very showy and colourful

(e) e _ pec _   to look forward to something that is likely to happen

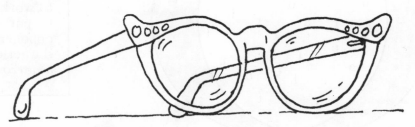

4 Alphabetical

Rearrange the words in the list so that they are in strictly alphabetical order.

5 Separate the footballs

Six words from the list are hidden in the footballs. However, the letters that begin and end the words are shown around the edges of the footballs. Find the six list words.

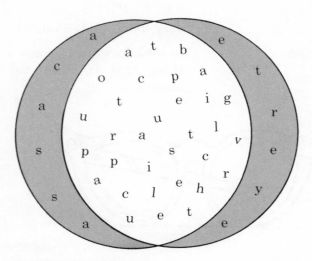

6 Same word — different meaning

One word can sometimes have more than one meaning. Write down all the list words below, then put in their different meanings.

Here's a 'meaning pool' for you to choose your meanings from.

an opportunity or chance for action
a kind of ticket
a large bus
a bad smell, dirty conditions
to spice
a person who trains a team or a player
to cut into or scratch something
the number of points won in a game
to allow to go by
to arrange or set out food
the time of the year when a game is mostly played
an unfair action against the rules in a game
a break or gap, an entrance
to work for a group or have a duty to do
to put the ball into play by hitting it to your opponent
the action of one player getting the ball to another
a narrow way across mountains

(a) foul   (1)_____
                 (2)_____

(b) season   (1)_____
                 (2)_____

(c) coach   (1)_____
                 (2)_____

(d) score   (1)_____
                 (2)_____

(e) opening   (1)_____
                 (2)_____

(f) serve   (1)_____
                 (2)_____
                 (3)_____

(g) pass   (1)_____
                 (2)_____
                 (3)_____
                 (4)_____

7 Words within words

See which word wins the quantity race. Find words within these words. One example has been given for you.

Applause	Accurate	Selected
plus	cure	tee

8 Spaceways

Complete the words from the list by building letters around either the vowel (a, e, i, o, u) or consonant (any of the other 21 letters of the alphabet).

_ _ e _ _ _ _ _ _ _   _ _ _ _ e

_ _ _ p _ _ _ _ _ _   _ _ _ _ l _ _ _

_ _ _ g _ _   _ _ _ _ r _

_ _ _ _ n _ _ _   _ _ u _ _ _

l	s	c	a	_	e
_	_	_	s	_	_
_		_		_	_
_		_		_	_
_				_	
_					

OBSERVE	BEAUTY	
VIEW	ATTRACTIVE	
NOTICE	UGLY	
EXAMINE	GLASSES	
DISCOVER	SEARCH	
RECOGNIZE	STARE	
ATTENTIVELY	SURVEY	
VISIBLE	GLANCE	
REGARD	LENS	
SIGHT	MICROSCOPE	

10 Looking and Seeing

1 Noun making

Change into nouns.

(a) observe	(b) visible
(c) ugly	(d) discover
(e) attentively	(f) recognize
(g) examine	(h) attractive

2 Participles

Complete the table.

	observe	observing	observed
(a)	regard		
(b)	glance		
(c)	survey		
(d)	search		
(e)	notice		

3 Opposites

Add prefixes to the following words to form their opposites.

(a) attractive	(b) visible
(c) recognizable	(d) regard
(e) attentive	(f) observant

4 Square words

Five of your list words are hidden in the squares below. The first letter of each word is hidden in the first square, the second letter is hidden in the second square, etc. Unscramble the words.

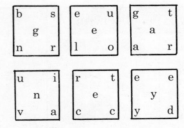

5 Verbs

Change to verbs.

(a) beauty	(b) attentively
(c) attractive	

6 Describers

Change to adjectives.

(a) beauty	(b) recognize
(c) notice	(d) microscope
(e) attentively	

7 Starters

The first two letters of some list words are written below. Complete the words.

(a) ug	(b) le
(c) mi	(d) ex
(e) si	(f) di
(g) no	(h) su

8 Crossword

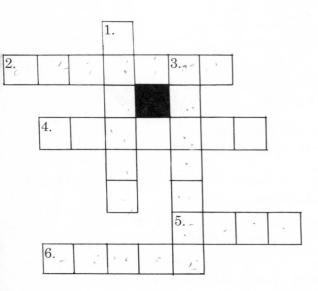

CLUES

1. To take notice of
2. To watch or become conscious of
3. Able to be seen
4. These help people with poor sight
5. Curved piece of glass
6. To look fixedly at an object

11 TRANSPORT

STATION	FLIGHT
AIRPORT	GUARD
AEROPLANE	FREIGHT
TICKET	AMBULANCE
CAPTAIN	ENGINE
PILOT	INSPECTOR
HELICOPTER	MOTORIST
STEWARD	PASSENGER
OFFICER	FERRY
HOSTESS	CARGO

1 Brackets

Complete the following sentences using the correct form of the word in brackets.

(a) The helicopter .... low over the flooded area. [flight]

(b) Modern man relies largely on the .... car for transport. [motorist]

(c) The .... of treasurer will be filled after an election next week. [officer]

(d) The mechanic will .... my car for rust. [inspector]

(e) The .... way between the shops was dirty and dark. [passenger]

2 Fill in

Every third letter of your list word is given. Complete the words.

(a) _ _ s _ _ s _   (b) _ _ a _ _

(c) _ _ a _ _ o _   (d) _ _ g _ _ e

(e) _ _ p _ _ i _   (f) _ _ e _ _ h _

(g) _ _ r _ _   (h) _ _ l _ _ o _ _ e _

3 Code

A=1, B=2, C=3, D=4, E=5, F=6, G=7, H=8, I=9, J=10, K=11, L=12, M=13, N=14, O=15, P=16, Q=17, R=18, S=19, T=20, U=21, V=22, W=23, X=24, Y=25, Z=26.

Decode the following.

(a) 1, 9, 18, 16, 15, 18, 20

(b) 19, 20, 5, 23, 1, 18, 4

(c) 3, 1, 18, 7, 15

(d) 20, 9, 3, 11, 5, 20

(e) 16, 9, 12, 15, 20

(f) 1, 5, 18, 15, 16, 12, 1, 14, 5

(g) 7, 21, 1, 18, 4

(h) 15, 6, 6, 9, 3, 5, 18

4 Blank it in

Insert the following words in the appropriate blank spaces.

station	flight
stewardess	motorist
aeroplane	passengers
engine	guard
tickets	

(a) The .... took off smoothly for New Zealand. The .... welcomed the .... on board and checked their ....

(b) A .... needs to fill his car with petrol at a service .... He must .... against his .... becoming overheated on a long journey.

5 More than one

Change to plural.

(a) aeroplane	(b) hostess
(c) ferry	(d) inspector
(e) cargo	

6 Jumbled sentences

Unscramble the following sentences.

(a) Passengers' the checked tickets inspector the.

(b) A land small in helicopter can a area.

(c) Scene to of raced accident the ambulances the.

(d) Liked the captain by was ship's passengers the.

(e) An lives of aeroplane may crash hundreds claim.

(f) Have a maintenance engine should car constant.

7 Action

Change into verbs.

(a) motorist	(b) flight
(c) inspector	(d) officer

8 Crossword

CLUES

1. Person who navigates a ship.
2. A woman who entertains guests.
3. Passengers' attendant and waiter on ship.
4. Freight of ship.
5. Pass to and fro over a river.

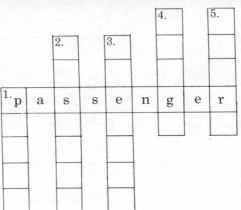

CHEERFUL	FRIGHTEN
ANNOYED	FUNNY
CONFIDENT	SATISFIED
NERVOUS	JEALOUS
SELFISH	SERIOUS
DECENT	HATRED
FRIENDLY	INTERESTING
DESPAIR	SUFFER
SORROW	GRIEF
DELIGHT	FATAL

12 Attitudes

1 Change it

Look at the word in brackets at the end of each sentence. Write down the correct form of the word in the blank spaces.

(a) He was the .... dog I had ever seen. [friendly]

(b) The teacher received no .... from the pupil's essay. [satisfied]

(c) The boy was .... when he lost control of the bike. [frighten]

(d) The burglar was charged with causing .... bodily harm. [grief]

(e) The actor .... said his lines. [nervous]

(f) Jimmy Connors .... hit a forehand winner. [confident]

(g) There was another .... on the road. [fatal]

(h) The dog was .... the young girl. [annoy]

2 Many parts

Fill in the following table. The first one has been done for you.

	NOUN	ADJECTIVE	VERB	ADVERB
	satisfaction	satisfying	satisfies	satisfactorily
(a)	grief			
(b)		interesting		
(c)				hastily
(d)		nervous		
(e)		funny		
(f)		fatal		
(g)	sorrow			
(h)			frightens	
(i)			despair	
(j)		serious		
(k)		selfish		

3 Link up

Make up list words from the two columns below.

(a) cheer   pair

(b) jeal   ish

(c) des   ful

(d) fat   light

(e) satis   ous

(f) self   al

(g) interest   fied

(h) de   ing

4 Match the meanings

(a) annoyed   not considerate of others

(b) fatal   a loss of hope

(c) satisfied   irritated

(d) delight   easily agitated, highly strung

(e) nervous   deep sorrow

(f) grief   great pleasure

(g) despair   ending in death

(h) selfish   contented

5 Happy and Unhappy

Draw up two columns in your book with the headings *Happy Words* and *Unhappy Words*. Then write down the words from your spelling list under these headings.

6 Missing

Fill in the missing letters.

(a) _ _ _ e _ _ u _

(b) _ u _ _ y

(c) _ e _ p _ _ _

(d) _ a _ r _ _

(e) _ e _ _ o _ _

(f) _ a _ a _

(g) _ _ i e _

(h) _ e _ e _ _

7 Word circle

The letters of three words from the list have been mixed up in the circle. What are the three words?

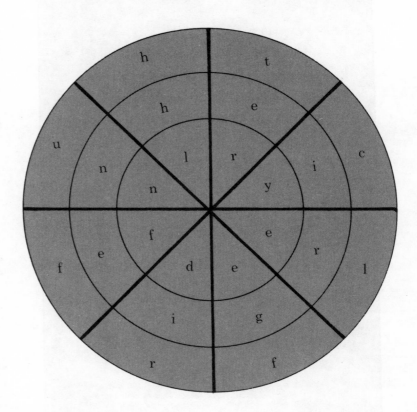

13 Bikes

BICYCLE	CONTROL
MIRROR	BALANCE
PEDAL	BRAKE
SPEED	STEEL
CYCLIST	ADJUST
GEAR	RACING
AXLE	REFLECTOR
TYRE	CHAIN
SHINING	VALVE
HANDLEBAR	STEER

1 Same words — with a difference

(a) Everyone knows that the GEAR on a bike is a little piece of machinery that makes it easier to pedal up hill. What other meaning does the word GEAR have?

(b) The same goes for STEER. See if you can give two meanings.

2 Same sound but different spelling, different meaning

(a) Change BRAKE to a word that means 'smash' by altering the position of two letters.

(b) Change TYRE to a word that means 'to get weary' by changing one letter.

(c) Change STEEL to a word that means 'take' by changing one letter.

3 Swerve through

this, putting in the missing letters of words from the list as you go.

s _ _ _ _ _ _
_ d _ _ _ _ _ _
_ _ i _ _ _ _ _ _ _ _
_ _ _ r _ _ _
_ _ _ 'c _ _ _ _ _
_ _ _ c _ _ _
_ _ _ _ b _ _

4 Linkups

Some of the list words are often linked with certain other words and phrases. Given a word or phrase below, find the list word.

_ _ _ _ _ grease

rear-vision _ _ _ _ _ _

_ _ _ _ _ _ pusher

_ _ _ _ _ _ demon

three-speed _ _ _ _

flat _ _ _ _

front-wheel _ _ _ _ _

tyre _ _ _ _ _ _

rear _ _ _ _ _ _ _ _ _

racing _ _ _ _ _ _ _ _ _ _ _

_ _ _ _ _ sprocket

5 -able

'Able' is a suffix (a group of letters that may be fixed to the end of a word) that gives the meaning of 'able to' or 'capable of'.

Find three words from the list that have the meanings given below.

Put each one in front of 'able'. Note that one of them has to add another 'l' before its suffix.

(a) _____ able   able to be directed or guided while on the move

(b) _____ lable   capable of being taken charge of

(c) _____ able   able to be fitted better

6 RE and BI

RE in front of a word usually gives the idea of 'back' or 'again' to the word's meaning. BI in front of a word gives the idea of 'two'.

(a) Find two words in the list that begin with RE and BI.

(b) Write down the meaning of each of these words, bringing in the idea of 'back' and 'two'.

(c) Find out at least five other words that begin with RE and five that begin with BI.

(d) Put them in sentences to show you know what they mean.

7   Putting the sense into sentences

From the words shown below, choose the word that fits the sense of each of the sentences.

(a) A little work with a spanner and the [pedalling, pedals, pedal] were working as well as they ever had.

(b) A small [adjustment, adjust, adjusting] was needed to correct the twist on the handlebars.

(c) The bike skidded as he was [brake, braking, braked] on a downhill run.

(d) In the sunlight, the mirror [shine, shone, shining] with an eye-aching dazzle.

(e) She showed great skill in her [controlling, control, controller] of the bike.

8 Wheeling words

A word from the list has been scattered around in each wheel. Work out the words and write them down letter by letter in the spaces. ('a' is in the innermost wheel, and so on outwards.)

(a) _ _ _ _ _ _ _

(b) _ _ _ _ _ _ _ _ _

(c) _ _ _ _ _ _ _ _

(d) _ _ _ _ _ _ _

(e) _ _ _ _ _ _ _

(f) _ _ _ _ _ _ _ _ _

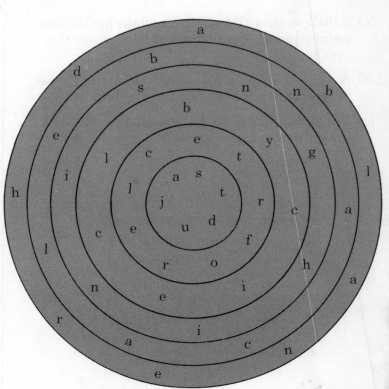

DECORATE	CURTAIN
PICTURE	PILLOW
CARPET	ENTRANCE
FURNITURE	LOUNGE
STAIRS	FIREPLACE
WINDOW	LAUNDRY
STOREY	GARBAGE
LADDER	DRAWER
KITCHEN	CUPBOARD
CEILING	BOOKSHELVES

14 At Home

1 Alphabetical

Rearrange these words into the order in which they would occur in the dictionary.

furniture	window
kitchen	fireplace
curtain	carpet
garbage	cupboard
ceiling	drawer

2 Clues

Use these clues to help you identify objects in your list.

(a) An object most likely to be found in the toolshed.

(b) The study would be untidy without some of these.

(c) Found hanging on a wall.

(d) One is part of the other. (Two words from the list)

(e) Not very likely to be in use in summer.

(f) Probably in a bin just outside the back door.

(g) Found in the bedroom.

(h) Without it you couldn't get in.

(i) A fly could walk on it, but you couldn't.

(j) Usually made of attractive material.

3 Pairs or pears

Each of the following pairs of words contains one word from your list and another word which sounds the same but has a different meaning. Choose the correct word to fit into the blank space in each sentence.

STOREY — STORY

(a) The lift took us up to the top .... of the tall building.

(b) The teacher read the first paragraph of the .... to the class.

CEILING — SEALING

(c) The man was .... the roof to prevent rain from getting in.

(d) The balloon bumped against the .... before coming back down.

STAIRS — STARES

(e) The lady with the funny hat attracted lots of .... from the people in the street.

(f) We walked up the .... and gazed at the beautiful view.

4 Endings and beginnings

Put each ending from the first column with its correct beginning from the second column, in order to find the following list words.

ENDINGS	BEGINNINGS
(a) pet	decor
(b) tain	car
(c) place	garb
(d) age	en
(e) ate	lad
(f) board	fire
(g) trance	pil
(h) der	cup
(i) low	furn
(j) iture	cur

5 A suspense story

Fill in the blanks in the following story with appropriate words from your list.

It was a cold night so I sat near the .... with my head resting on a .... I was looking at the .... hanging on the wall above the .... where I kept the encyclopaedias. Suddenly I heard a thump on the .... above me. We have a two .... house and I knew I was the only one at home. I tiptoed across the .... and into the .... to get a knife from the .... Then going back through the .... I slowly began to mount the .... Imagine my relief when I saw what had happened. Apparently a cat had come through the open .... , and knocked over a small .... which I had been using to help me .... the room.

6 Spell-a-word

For this spelling game, divide the class into pairs. Draw up score pads in your workbook like the one below.

(1) Player 1 chooses a word from the list for his partner (player 2) to spell. If it is spelt correctly, player 2 earns a point. If spelt incorrectly, player 1 earns the point. Points are scored in the player's column on the score pad.

(2) In turn, player 2 now chooses a word from the list and asks player 1 to spell it. Scoring is the same.

(3) Note any errors as they occur. When all the words have been asked, each player has one minute to review any words he has spelt incorrectly. After one minute, player 1 asks player 2 to spell the errors that he has just reviewed. Then player 2 asks player 1 to spell his earlier errors again.

(4) Scoring in this latter section is doubled. For every correct word the speller receives two points. For every error made by the person spelling, the asker receives two points.

Total the points to find the winner.

7 Front or back

Use these clues to help you find words from your list. Here is an example.

First part is a vehicle. Answer: *carpet*

(a) First part is a woolly coat.

(b) Begins with a tablet.

(c) Ends with the opposite of wet.

(d) Begins with a shop.

(e) Ends with something we breathe.

(f) Begins with a little boy.

(g) Ends with a number of years.

(h) Ends with little fairy folk.

8 Gaps

Fill in the gaps to make words from the list.

(a) _a_n_r_

(b) _u_b_a_d

(c) l_u_g_

(d) _i_c_en

(e) _a_d_r

(f) _i_d_w

(g) _e_o_a_e

(h) _e_l_n

15 THE BOOK

PRINTER	CONTENTS
PUBLISHER	REFERENCE
AUTHOR	SPELLING
TYPING	TITLE
SENTENCE	EDITOR
PARAGRAPH	PREFACE
CHAPTER	MARGIN
BINDING	PHOTOGRAPH
COMMA	INDEX
DRAWING	DESIGN

1 Countdown

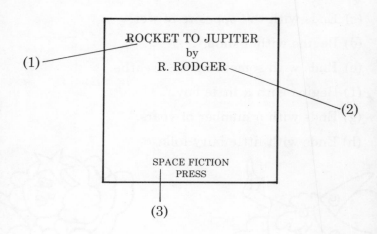

Put down the words from the spelling list that describe:

(1) _ _ _ _ _ _

(2) _ _ _ _ _ _

(3) _ _ _ _ _ _ _ _ _

2 Boxed in

The first letters of five words are in the outer box.
Their last letters are in the inner box. Work out the
five words from the list.

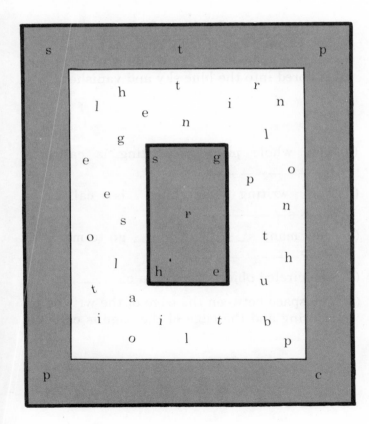

3 Cover to cover

Front cover

(a)

(b)

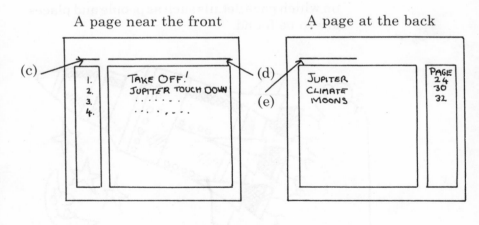

A page near the front

A page at the back

(c)

(d)

(e)

Note the arrows with letters attached that point to the book pages shown. Each of the letters begins a statement with a space. Fill in each space with a word from the list. The number of letters in each word is shown.

(a) The _ _ _ _ _ _ _ holds the book together.

(b) The front cover has a dramatic _ _ _ _ _ _ .

(c) Each main section of a book is called a _ _ _ _ _ _ _ _ .

(d) The book's table of _ _ _ _ _ _ _ _ is usually placed just before the story.

(e) Some books have an _ _ _ _ _ _ that tells you on which page details such as people and places are to be found.

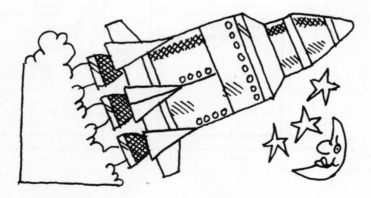

4   Playing with fire

Here's how *Rocket To Jupiter* begins:

'A great tail of fire leapt from the end of the rocket. Crowds cheered, TV cameras zoomed. The rocket rose⊙ slowly at first, then faster and faster till it bored into the blue sky and vanished.'

(a) This whole piece of writing is called a p_ _ _ _ _ _ _ _ _ .

(b) The writing underlined is called a s_ _ _ _ _ _ _ _ .

(c) How many s_ _ _ _ _ _ _ _ _ go to make up the p_ _ _ _ _ _ _ _ _ ?

(d) The circled object is called a c_ _ _ _ _ _ .

(e) The space between the edge of the writing or printing and the edge of the page is called a m_ _ _ _ _ _ .

5 One across — three down

Four important people in the production of a book are:

```
              3.
              _
              _
       2.     _  4.
       _      _  _
 1. _ u _ _ o r
       _      _  _
       _         _
       _         _
       _         _
       _
       _
```

CLUES

1. The person who writes the book.
2. The person who arranges and issues the book.
3. The person who checks and corrects.
4. The person who prints the final letters on the page.

6 Word swamp

Five words from the list have been swamped in letters.

MARGIN   COMMA   CONTENTS

REFERENCE PREFACE

Look for them across, up and down, and at a slant. Copy the grid and shade the letters.

l	c	n	l	p	t	i	g	r	w	y	n
c	m	o	a	c	s	n	i	d	r	w	t
p	o	m	t	d	m	o	n	m	a	l	i
t	e	n	i	p	a	d	w	f	m	a	t
c	o	n	t	r	i	a	n	s	b	i	l
e	d	r	r	e	f	e	r	e	n	c	e
m	b	o	n	f	n	w	s	n	p	t	s
o	a	c	m	a	b	t	a	e	h	w	f
t	b	r	t	c	r	i	s	t	g	n	a
p	c	h	g	e	o	e	s	c	w	g	c
t	s	h	o	i	n	m	g	b	d	f	e
m	o	r	e	l	n	b	m	r	a	c	d
f	c	d	o	m	l	c	b	a	s	a	t

7 People and jobs

The following words from the list can be added to downwards to give either a person or a job activity.

One letter of each word is given to you. All you have to do is write down the letters you would put in the circles. (Note the clues in brackets!)

○yping

○
○
○
○
○

(A person who does typing is a ....?)

dr○wing

○
○
○
○
○

(A person who does drawing is an ....?)

○hotograph

○
○
○
○
○
○
○
○
○
○

○esign

○
○
○
○
○
○

(The person who takes the photograph is a ....?)

(The person who does the design is a ....?)

○ublisher

○
○
○
○
○
○
○
○
○
○

(He or she works at ....?)

○ditor

○
○
○
○

(He or she ....a book?)

autho○

○
○
○
○
○

(He or she .... a book?)

8 Ifs

Try fitting each of these words into its correct slot in the sentences below.

typing	preface	binding
design	reference	

(a) If you like the drawing, colours and words on the cover of a book, you'll know you're attracted by the ....

(b) If your handwriting looks like old barbed wire, you'd better try .... instead.

(c) If there's a fact or other piece of information you want to find·out about, look up a .... book.

(d) If you want to be told, briefly, what a book is all about, turn to the first few pages of the book and read the ....

(e) If a book looks like falling apart, it probably needs a new ....

Spellbound's Noughts and Crosses Game

RULES

(1) The teacher (or a class member) draws up onto the blackboard a noughts and crosses grid, one metre by one metre.

(2) The teacher gives each of the nine squares a topic taken from the spelling units in this book. For each new game, the topics are rubbed out and new ones inserted.

(3) Each member of the class (except for the two contestants) is allocated a topic from the spelling book, and should turn to the appropriate page so that the contestants can be asked to spell words from the list.

(4) One of the best ways of playing the game is to divide the class into two teams. Then for each game, a contestant is selected from each group. The names of the contestants who are to play against each other in a game can be taken from a hat.

(5) *The Game Begins*

First of all, the two contestants select a piece of chalk. They are going to play a game of noughts and crosses, but they will only be allowed to put up a nought or cross when they spell a word correctly. The teacher tosses a coin to see who will go first and the person who wins the toss will chalk up crosses and the opponent will chalk up noughts. The contestant who is having first go selects his topic (e.g. *Thinking*) from the grid. The student in the class who is looking after *Thinking* asks the contestant a word from the *Thinking* list. If the contestant spells the word correctly, a cross is put in the *Thinking* box in the grid. If the contestant spells the word incorrectly, no cross is allowed. Whatever happens, it now becomes the noughts contestant's turn, and the same process is repeated. Obviously, a box with a cross or a nought in it cannot be used again. A box without a nought or cross can be used until one of the contestants is able to spell its word correctly. Succeed or fail, each contestant is allowed only one go at a time, as in noughts and crosses. Let the game begin!

SANDWICH	SAUCE
BUTTER	LAMB
SUGAR	BOTTLE
KNIFE	LOAF
MARGARINE	DINNER
DESSERT	COFFEE
BREAKFAST	SAUSAGE
BOILING	VEGETABLE
BREAD	STEAK
ROAST	CEREAL

16 Meal Time

1 Missing words

Write out the sentences below and insert the correct form of the word in brackets.

(a) The cook .... the sausages. [boiling]

(b) His wife was .... the lamb for dinner. [roast]

(c) Their family .... well at the new restaurant. [dinner]

(d) The guest at the hotel .... his bread. [butter]

(e) The company had .... vast quantities of lemonade. [bottle]

(f) Most .... have a pleasant taste. [dessert]

2 Jumbled sentences

Rearrange the following words into sentences that have meaning.

(a) For sauce the with manager lamb had his dinner.

(b) with bread margarine student spread his a knife on the.

(c) coffee the boiling served was

(d) used sauce of the breakfast bottle was at.

(e) Dinner there and for vegetables were steak.

(f) spread cereal she her on sugar.

3 Rules for making plurals

For most nouns, just add 's'. Examples: boy—boys; girl—girls.

When words end in 'ch', 's', 'sh' and 'x', add 'es'. Examples: lunch—lunches; bus—buses; wish—wishes; box—boxes. (N.B. ox—oxen.)

Many words that end in 'f' or 'fe' change the 'f' to 'v' before adding 'es' to make the plural. Examples: leaf—leaves; wolf—wolves.

Form the plural of the following words.

	List Words		Other Words For Practice
(a)	sandwich	(k)	cross
(b)	knife	(l)	church
(c)	roast	(m)	express
(d)	breakfast	(n)	wharf
(e)	dessert	(o)	bunch
(f)	sauce	(p)	half
(g)	bottle	(q)	thief
(h)	loaf	(r)	calf
(i)	sausage	(s)	march
(j)	lamb	(t)	wife

4 Words that sound the same

Write the sentences and use the correct words from the brackets.

(a) .... is not usually served in the .... [dessert, desert]

(b) As he listened to his radio .... , he ate his .... [cereal, serial]

(c) He was .... in Australia, which produces enough .... for its people. [bread, bred]

(d) The supermarket had discovered a reliable .... of tomato .... [sauce, source]

(e) Because the butchers had gone on strike, our supply of .... was at .... [steak, stake]

5 Cracking the code

Take the shape formed by the lines around the letters as a code; e.g. R= ⎵ , D= ☐ .

A	R	E
B	D	S
C	T	U

Now decode the following to form words from your list.

(a) ☐⎵⊏⊏⎵⎵⊓
(b) ⊐⌐⌐⎵⎵⎵⎵
(c) ⊐⎵⎵⎴⊐
(d) ⊏⊐⌐⌐⎵

6 Magic squares

There are five words from the list hidden in the squares below. The first letter of each word is hidden in the first square, the second letter is hidden in the second square, and so on. Find out what the five words are.

7 Scrambled letters

Unscramble the mixed-up letters to form words in the list.

(a) s r e b a f t k a	(e) n r e n d i
(b) t u b t r e	(f) k e s t a
(c) e i f n k	(g) r e d a b
(d) r n i e a a g m r	(h) l e r e c a

8 Silent letters

You have already noticed that the 'k' in knife is not pronounced. Below is a list of words that have a silent 'k'. Fill in the missing letters to form the words. Sometimes you can make up more than one word.

(a) kn__e   (b) kn__w

(c) kn__t   (d) kn__gh__

(e) kn__ck   (f) kn__ckle

(g) kn__wledg__   (h) kn__lt

(i) kn__b

CROWD	RELATION
GROUP	INFANT
HUSBAND	WIFE
GUEST	FEMALE
NEIGHBOUR	YOUTH
MOTHER	CHILDREN
BROTHER	PRIVATE
DAUGHTER	STRANGER
COUSIN	GENTLEMAN
PARENT	BACHELOR

1 Male & female

Write down the female form of the following words. The first one has been done for you.

(a)	male	female
(b)	husband	
(c)	brother	
(d)	uncle	
(e)	gentleman	
(f)	bachelor	
(g)	son	
(h)	father	
(i)	man	
(j)	nephew	

2 The right word in the right place

Choose the right word for the right place in the following sentences.

(a) .... I think the .... where I live is uninteresting. [private, privately, privacy/ neighbourly, neighbours, neighbourhood]

(b) The responsibility of .... often improves the .... between a man and woman. [relationship, relative, related, relation, parents, parental, parenthood, parent]

3 Backwards or scrambled

These list words have either been written backwards or have had their letters scrambled. Work out the words.

meltnage	fitnan
rehtorb	rolehcab
dabnush	etavirp
tseug	ganrets
rapten	hoytu
elamef	noitaler

4 One little word

Rewrite these sentences, using a word from the spelling list where you can instead of some of the phrases. (A phrase is a little group of words.)

She was married to him. She was his wife.

(a) John lives next door to me.

(b) Mary is my aunt's child.

(c) He is staying at our place.

(d) He is the man who is married to my sister.

(e) I do not know her.

(f) She sings with several other people.

(g) The 8-year-old felt lost among the large numbers of people.

(h) He was only about 16 years old.

(i) They had grown a high hedge round their place so that people would not keep peering in at them.

5 Hard-to-find family

Search for these family words lost in the letters below.

daughter	mother
infant	husband
brother	wife

m	o	u	a	h	o	t	w	h	i
p	c	b	f	t	m	o	i	r	n
h	d	a	u	g	h	t	e	r	f
b	p	b	s	b	g	h	d	o	a
g	a	b	r	r	t	t	a	e	n
r	h	u	r	o	e	g	h	n	t
t	h	l	m	n	t	m	i	h	n
e	u	r	f	m	o	h	d	u	c
w	s	o	a	w	i	f	e	b	f
n	b	a	n	d	g	o	n	r	r

6 o

Below is a large 'o' shared by words from the list. Fill in the words.

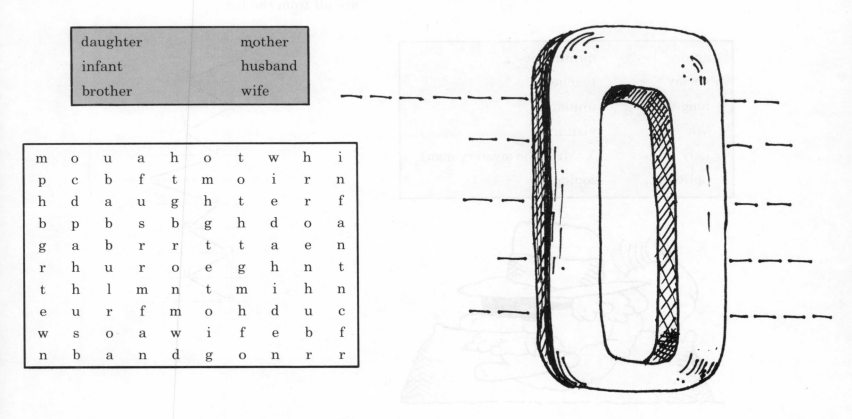

7 A—Z

Rearrange the spelling list alphabetically, including these extra words as you go.

actor	quintuplet
enemy	teacher
judge	unionist
kin	visitor
lady	X (Mr X the mystery man)
optician	zoologist

8 Person to person

The line leads from person to person and gives you the only letter you've got! Find the words—they are all from the list.

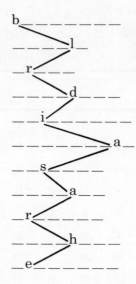

QUIETLY   FORTUNATELY

EASILY   THOROUGHLY

FINALLY   URGENTLY

GRADUALLY   ALREADY

CAREFULLY   ANNUALLY

HURRIEDLY   ONLY

USUALLY   QUICKLY

HAPPILY   ENTIRELY

SUDDENLY   RARELY

ACTUALLY   IMMEDIATELY

18 Ways of Doing Things

1 Word families

Copy and complete the following word family table. The first one is completed for you.

	ADVERB	ADJECTIVE	NOUN
(a)	quietly	quiet	quietness
(b)	carefully	....	....
(c)	happily	....	....
(d)	quickly	....	....
(e)	easily	....	....
(f)	thoroughly	....	....
(g)	urgently	....	....
(h)	fortunately	....	....

2 Words and their meanings

The following list words are surrounded by several possible meanings, only one of which is correct. Identify the correct meaning in each case.

scattered all over with a gentle manner completely	(a) thoroughly	in a rough way without much thought angrily
clearly in a shocking way like a pest	(b) gradually	slowly, one bit at a time with a lot of trouble with a lot of heat
making a lot of noise safely without fear	(c) urgently	happening very often different from all others in a way that calls for immediate attention
done with the hands happening once each year flashing through the mind	(d) annually	forcefully without any questions wrongly
in a natural way breathing deeply safely and surely	(e) rarely	cautiously not happening very often sadly

3 Alphabetical

Rearrange these list words in the order in which they would be found in a dictionary.

hurriedly	quickly
easily	happily
gradually	actually
already	quietly
rarely	usually

4 Meaning sentences

Use each of the following list words in sentences of your own.

(a) immediately	(b) entirely
(c) fortunately	(d) only
(e) usually	(f) actually

5 Secret code

Solve the following code and discover what each list word is. The only clue you are given to help you solve the code is that the letters 'm' and 'z' on the end of each word stand for 'l' and 'y' respectively.

(a) gjobmmz	(b) ibqqjmz
(c) jnnfejbufmz	(d) tveefomz
(e) foujsfmz	(f) ivssjefmz
(g) vtvbmmz	(h) bduvbmmz
(i) dbsfgvmmz	(j) bmsfbez

6 Criss-crossword

Copy the criss-crossword below into your workbooks. Then use the clues to solve it. Each word is from your list.

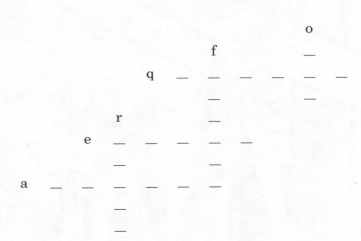

CLUES

Q: Carried out with a lot of speed
F: Lastly
E: Carried out without any trouble
R: Only happening very occasionally
O: You .... live once
A: By this time

7 Got the clues?

Identify, and write out, the list words suggested by the following clues.

(a) This word is 'rough' in the middle.

(b) This word has a 'den' in the middle.

(c) Starts with 'on'.

(d) This word has a 'gent' in the middle.

(e) This word has a backwards 'tan' in the middle.

(f) Rhymes with 'barely'.

(g) This word starts with 'us'.

(h) This word has a backwards 'lip' in the middle.

(i) This word has a jumbled 'dear' in the middle.

(j) Rhymes with 'prickly'.

8 Unscramble the letters

Below are words from the list with their letters mixed up. Write down the words.

(a) y i f l a n l	(e) l a s e i y
(b) r l a d y e a	(f) l a s y l u u
(c) a y i p h p l	(g) a e r y l r
(d) l e t n e i y r	(h) y r h l e u r d i

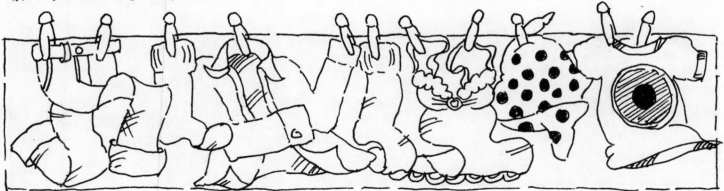

HEATER	STEREO
RADIATOR	TRANSISTOR
KETTLE	RECORDER
TOASTER	TELEVISION
DRYER	TELEPHONE
SEWING MACHINE	STOVE
WASHING MACHINE	POLISHER
AIR CONDITIONER	OVEN
VACUUM CLEANER	GRILLER
DISH WASHER	BEDLAMP

19 Appliances in the Home

1 Got the clues?

Choose an appliance from the list to fit each clue.

(a) Handy on a wet washing day.

(b) Used more in the winter months.

(c) Saves you getting out of bed to switch lights on or off.

(d) Does a lot of the work for you after a meal.

(e) You usually put bread into this.

(f) Is used when the weather is really hot.

(g) Makes and repairs clothes.

(h) Helps your friends to keep in touch.

(i) Puts the shine on things.

(j) The place where a baked dinner is cooked.

2 ABC

Write the following words out in the order in which they would occur in a dictionary.

washing machine	recorder
stereo	telephone
dryer	kettle
dishwasher	radiator
television	vacuum cleaner

3 Missing letters

Every third letter of the following list words is provided. Fill in the missing letters.

_ _ c _ _ d _ _   _ _ l _ _ h _ _ e

_ _ a _ _ e _   _ _ l _ _ i _ _ o _

_ _ i _ _ e _   _ _ c _ _ m _ _ e _ _ r _

_ _ a _ _ i _ _ o _

4 Room service

Copy the diagrams into your workbook, and write the name of each appliance into the appropriate room—the room where it is usually found in the house.

APPLIANCES

oven	griller
dish washer	stove
stereo	kettle
television	washing machine
dryer	toaster

lounge/living room

kitchen

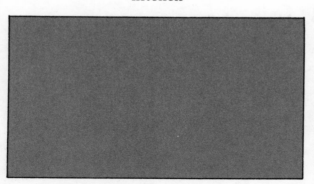

laundry

5 Why

Explain in your own words:

(a) why a vacuum cleaner is called a *vacuum cleaner*

(b) the difference between a griller and a gorilla

(c) why an air conditioner is called an air *conditioner*

(d) why most record players are called stereos

6 Picture story

Identify the following list words.

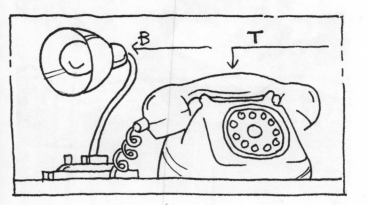

7 Word salad

In the word salad below, seven words from the list are hidden. They may be written forwards or backwards, up or down (but not diagonally). Find the seven words.

a	b	n	e	v	o	d	c
d	r	e	l	l	i	r	g
e	v	o	t	s	e	y	f
h	e	a	t	e	r	e	g
o	e	r	e	t	s	r	h
i	j	s	k	m	r	y	l

8 Match up the endings

Make up words from your list by selecting the correct parts from each column.

(a)	dry	le
(b)	toast	en
(c)	radiat	er
(d)	ov	or
(e)	transist	phone
(f)	tele	er
(g)	kett	or

SANDALS	STYLE
SHOES	SUIT
PANTS	HANDKERCHIEF
DRESS	CLOTHING
COAT	WEARING
SHIRT	GOWN
SLEEVES	JEANS
PAIR	WOOLLEN
POCKET	MEASURE
NYLON	FASHION

20   What to Wear

1   Ends

(a) -ISH   -FUL   -ABLE   -MENT

These are some of the groups of letters that can be added to the ends of some words. They are called 'suffixes'. (Prefixes are added to the front of some words.) Now choose the correct suffix for each of these four words.

> MEASURE
> POCKET
> STYLE (the 'e' has to be dropped)
> FASHION

(b) Now fit the new words you have formed with suffixes into the passage below.

She looked .... in straight leg jeans which were also .... for that year. The tailor made a careful .... before selecting a pin from the .... he always carried.

2 'A' for attractive

Look at the list of spelling words. Then fill in the blanks.

```
_ _ a _
_ a _ _
_ a _ _ _ _
_ a _ _ a _ _
_ _ a _ _
_ a _ _ _ _ _ _ _ _ _
_ a _ _ _ _
```

3 'Sssssss'

Find the four words in the spelling list that have two 'esses' in them, and fit them into this hissing snake.

4 Scrambled words

Try tidying up this clothing by putting the letters in the right order. All the words are from the list.

(a) gawiren	(b) strih
(c) yonnl	(d) leonwol
(e) wogn	(f) vesseel
(g) sejan	(h) ceptok
(i) glinthoc	(j) tisu

5 What to wear

Here are ten words to fit into the crossword. The longest word has been filled in for you. See how you go with the other nine.

MEASURE POCKET JEANS SLEEVES COAT CLOTHING SHIRT SHOES NYLON HANDKERCHIEF

Crush it.

Punish it.

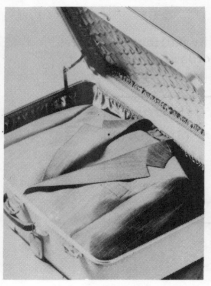

Pack it.

Squeeze it.

Do your worst.
In 'Euro-weave' you'll still look your best.

6   Web of words

In this exercise, pairs of words from the list have been oozed together and stuck in the web. Try releasing and separating them. The arrow points to an example, and here it is oozed out for you: SHOES—WOOLLEN. All the rest are yours!

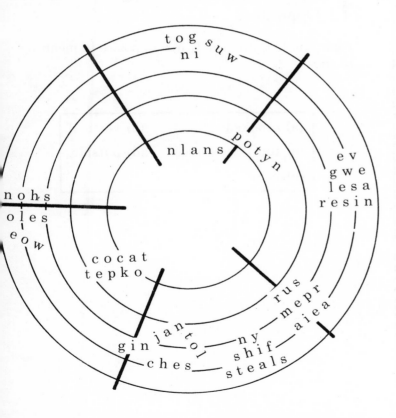

7   Let's take a commercial break

Work out the list words in this commercial.

THE *CHIC* GUYS N' GALS
brings YOU the latest
in _a_ _ _ _ _ _ wear!

For that DRESS-UP occasion: _u_ _s and
_ _ _ns.

For WORK-A-DAY wear: _e_ _s, _ _n_s,
and _ _i_ _s, and all other _ _ _ _ _es of
_ _l_ _ and _ _ _l_ _ _l_ _ _ _ _ _.

In our FOOTWEAR section we can offer you
_ _ _ _ _ _ _s and _ _o_ _

TAILORING SERVICE
We _ _ _ _ _u_ _ and _ _ _ _l_ to suit *your*
individual taste.
BUY HERE and WALK OUT
_ _ _ _ _ _n_ the BEST!

21 Shapes

SQUARE	HORIZONTAL
CIRCLE	DIAGONAL
CURVE	CENTRE
TRIANGLE	MIDDLE
DIAMOND	BOTTOM
STRAIGHT	DISTANT
CROOKED	BETWEEN
ANGLE	BEHIND
ROUND	BEYOND
VERTICAL	INSIDE

1 Opposites

From the list, find the words opposite in meaning to these.

(a) crooked	(b) vertical
(c) top	(d) outside
(e) near	

2 Mixup

Unscramble the following words from the list. Then take the letters that have been circled and make up another word.

(a) e s ⓤ r a q

(b) i d l m ⓔ d

(c) r e c ⓥ l a i t

(d) n o ⓡ d u

(e) o e o d ⓒ k r

3 Splits

Write down the left-hand column. Then make up a word from your list by attaching an ending from the right-hand column.

(a) dia	tween
(b) tri	side
(c) be	mond
(d) in	ical
(e) crook	angle
(f) vert	ed

4 Brackets

Complete the following sentences using the correct form of the word in brackets.

(a) The fisherman saw a ship on the .... [horizontal]

(b) The melon was .... in shape. [circle]

(c) The rocket took off .... [vertical]

(d) The satellite was .... earth. [circle]

(e) The school was .... in the community. [centre]

(f) There was a great .... to be covered. [distant]

(g) There were four .... in the window. [square]

(h) The painter hung the picture .... [crooked]

(i) The golf ball was .... towards the green. [curve]

5 Fill in

Find the words.

(a) _ _ r _ _ g _ _

(b) _ _ s _ _ e

(c) _ _ a _ _ n _ _

(d) _ _ n _ r _

(e) _ _ t _ o _

(f) _ i _ _ l _

(g) _ o _ n _

(h) _ _ a _ o _ _

6   Crack the code

A=1, B=2, C=3, D=4, E=5, F=6, G=7, H=8,
I=9, J=10, K=11, L=12, M=13, N=14, O=15,
P=16, Q=17, R=18, S=19, T=20, U=21, V=22,
W=23, X=24, Y=25, Z=26.

(a) 2, 5, 20, 23, 5, 5, 14

(b) 19, 17, 21, 1, 18, 5

(c) 8, 15, 18, 9, 26, 15, 14, 20, 1, 12

(d) 2, 5, 25, 15, 14, 4

(e) 3, 5, 14, 20, 18, 5

(f) 19, 20, 18, 1, 9, 7, 8, 20

(g) 2, 5, 8, 9, 14, 4

(h) 4, 9, 19, 20, 1, 14, 20

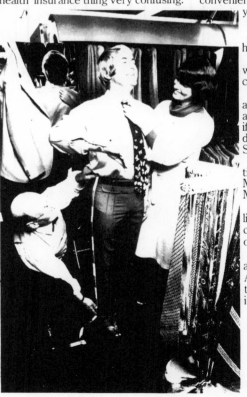

7 Magic box

In the first box look for the first letter of each of five words from your list. In the second box look for the second letter, and so on. Find the five words.

1		2		3		4		5		6	
m	c	o	q	n	d	d	t	l	r	e	e
s		i		u		c		r		e	
b	c	e	i	r	t	a	t	o	l	e	m

8 Where words come from

The Latin word *tri* means 'three'. A triangle has three angles. Next to the unfinished words below are their meanings. Fill in the blanks with the missing letters.

(a) tric _ _ le   having three wheels

(b) trip _ _ _ e   aeroplane with three wings

(c) tr _ p _ e _ s   set of three children

(d) tr _ p _ _ c _ te each of a set of three copies

(e) tr _ p _ d   three-legged stand for supporting a camera

(f) tr _ s _ lla _ _ e word of three syllables

(g) trim _ r _ n   a sailing boat with three hulls

(h) tric _ ps   large three-headed muscle at the back of the arm

(i) tr _ d _ nt   three-pronged fork often held by King Neptune

(j) trienni _ l   happening every three years

LARGE	AMOUNT
GIANT	INCREASE
NARROW	LENGTH
HEIGHT	REDUCE
GREAT	BREADTH
LITTLE	THICKNESS
SMALL	ENORMOUS
HEAVY	LITRE
HUGE	DEGREE
VOLUME	AREA

22 Size

1 Parts

Complete the following table.

	NOUN	ADJECTIVE	ADVERB
(a)		narrow	
(b)		heavy	
(c)	breadth		
(d)		great	
(e)	height		

Now Open

Western Plains Zoo, Dubbo

How about a day seeing the wild life of **Africa, Asia, America, Europe and Australia** soon.

It's possible now at Australia's greatest wild life park, the new Western Plains Zoo. Just five km from Dubbo P.O., you can now drive past herds of Bison, Deer and Giraffe. See Hippo, Camel and Monkeys in open-range areas closely simulating their natural environment. With only deep moat separating you from these magnificent range animals.

Stroll down bushland tracks to picnic sites, or use the free gas barbecue facilities for lunch. Then take the children to Friendship Farm where they can make friends with baby animals. Western Plains Zoo — the zoo without bars — is now open every day of the year from 9 a.m. Tel: Dubbo (STD) 068:82 5888.

2 Another form

Look at the words in italics in the following sentences. Then write down the word from the list from which they are formed.

(a) The road was *long* and winding.

(b) Toasting bread is *thicker* than sandwich bread.

(c) After the postal strike there was a *voluminous* amount of mail.

(d) The examination questions were *largely* practical.

(e) The cliff was too *high* to climb.

(f) The candidate was *narrowly* beaten by his opponent.

3 Front up

The last two letters of some list words are written below. Complete the words.

(a) nt (2 answers)	(b) le
(c) ea	(d) ll
(e) ce	(f) re
(g) us	(h) vy

4 Code

Every second letter of the following 'words' will form a list word. From each 'word' form two list words.

(a) n r a e r d r u o c w e

(b) i e n n c o r r e m a o s u e s

(c) h g e i a a v n y t

(d) h d e e i g g r h e t e

(e) a h r u e g a e

(f) s l m i a t l r l e

5 Meanings

The meanings of six list words are written below. Write down the words which match the meanings.

(a) to become greater or grow in number

(b) a metric unit of capacity equal to 1000 milli-litres

(c) a measure from side to side

(d) of great weight

(e) a person of huge build or stature

(f) not wide

6 Find the words

Hidden in the following table are nine of your list words. They occur in a *straight* line horizontally, vertically or diagonally, and some will read back-to-front.

h	e	i	g	h	t	h
e	a	m	o	u	n	t
a	r	r	i	g	t	d
v	s	d	e	e	c	a
y	g	r	e	a	t	e
e	c	u	d	e	r	r
d	e	g	r	e	e	b

7 Mixed bag

Unscramble the following list words.

(a) lamsl	(b) neescari
(c) telir	(d) greede
(e) nectkissh	(f) nagti
(g) moonsure	(h) creedu

TWO	DOZEN
EIGHT	PAIR
TWELVE	SINGLE
FORTY	SEVERAL
HUNDRED	AVERAGE
THOUSAND	ENOUGH
MILLION	NOTHING
QUARTER	NEITHER
MULTIPLY	ANOTHER
FIGURE	DOUBLE

23 Numbers

1,000,000,000,000,

1 Blanks

Fill in the missing list words.

(a) Eggs are bought in containers holding one d............ .

(b) I bought my mother a p............ of slippers for her birthday.

(c) One h............ years is called a century.

(d) In his will the millionaire left a q............ of a m............ dollars to his grandson.

(e) Her exam mark was well below a............ and n............ her mother nor her father was satisfied with the girl's performance.

(f) A t............ people flocked to the site of the air disaster which claimed f............ lives.

2 Join up

Write down the list on the left-hand side of your page. Then add the correct ending to each word from the endings in the other column.

(a)	for	ply
(b)	sever	ve
(c)	quart	ty
(d)	multi	gh
(e)	doub	er
(f)	enou	ion
(g)	mill	al
(h)	twel	le

3 Endings

Write all the words from your list ending with:

(a) 'le' and 'al'

(b) 'er' and 'ure'

4 Crossword

ACROSS
1. Not either
2. Humans have .... legs.
3. Number of cents in one dollar
5. One only
6. The Roman numeral for this number is XL

DOWN
1. Not anything
2. One hundred multiplied by ten
4. A spider has .... legs

5 Cracking the code

A=1, B=2, C=3, D=4, E=5, F=6, G=7, H=8,
I=9, J=10, K=11, L=12, M=13, N=14, O=15,
P=16, Q=17, R=18, S=19, T=20, U=21, V=22,
W=23, X=24, Y=25, Z=26.

Decode the following.

(a) 6, 9, 7, 21, 18, 5

(b) 19, 9, 14, 7, 12, 5

(c) 14, 15, 20, 8, 9, 14, 7

(d) 20, 8, 15, 21, 19, 1, 14, 4

(e) 19, 5, 22, 5, 18, 1, 12

(f) 20, 23, 5, 12, 22, 5

(g) 17, 21, 1, 18, 20, 5, 18

(h) 4, 15, 26, 5, 14

6 Circles and squares

Unscramble the following five words and write
them in the circles and squares. Then write down
the letters in the squares to form a sixth word.

(a) r e f i g u   □ ○ ○ ○ ○ ○

(b) h a o n r e t   ○ ○ □ ○ ○ ○ ○

(c) n u d e d r h   ○ ○ ○ ○ □ ○ ○

(d) w e t v e l   □ ○ ○ ○ ○ ○

(e) t i l l y p u m   ○ ○ ○ ○ ○ ○ ○ □

7 Er

Write down all the list words which have 'er' in
them.

24 Descriptive Words

SCARCE	POWERFUL
AWFUL	REGULAR
ALIVE	VARIOUS
CAPABLE	DIFFICULT
ARTIFICIAL	DIFFERENT
BRIEF	FIERCE
COMMON	GENUINE
HUNGRY	ALARMING
SENSIBLE	TIRED
ORDINARY	CONSCIOUS

1 Alphabetical

Rearrange the following list words into the order in which they would occur in a dictionary.

difficult	alive
tired	scarce
fierce	artificial
common	awful
ordinary	various

2 Fill in

Choose the most appropriate words from the list to complete each of the following sentences.

(a) He thought carefully about it, then made what seemed the most ....e decision.

(b) The .... dog gulped the meat down quickly.

(c) Food was so .... that people were selling all their possessions to buy it.

(d) The problem was too .... for all but the best mathematicians.

(e) The .... roses looked pretty but had no perfume.

(f) When a petrol strike occurs, ... customers are served first.

(g) The word that a hurricane was on the way came as an ....g piece of news for everyone.

(h) After the bump on the head he was not .... of what was happening.

(i) There are ....s ways of tackling the task.

(j) The car salesman assured him that the mileage on the car was ....

3 Join up

By putting the correct parts of words from columns 1, 2 and 3 together, form nine words which occur in your list. Use each part once only.

	1	2	3
(a)	dif	a	ble
(b)	pow	i	ine
(c)	reg	u	ent
(d)	var	fer	cult
(e)	gen	fi	ful
(f)	dif	u	cial
(g)	arti	in	ary
(h)	ord	fi	ous
(i)	cap	er	lar

4 Sentences

Create sentences of your own using each of the following list words.

(a) scarce	(b) sensible
(c) fierce	(d) awful
(e) powerful	(f) common
(g) ordinary	(h) brief
(i) tired	(j) conscious

5 Criss-crossword

Copy the criss-crossword below into your workbook. Then use the clues provided to help you solve it. Each word is from the list.

```
                              g
          c2                  —
          o   — — — — — — —
          —                  —
          —        s         —        t
          —        c  — — —  —  — — — — — —
          —                  —
          —                  —
          —                  —
     p    — — — — — — — —
```

CLUES

o: not at all unusual
g: not an imitation
c: aware of what is happening
c2: same clue as for 'o'
s: not many around
t: feeling weary
p: strong

6 Opposites

(a) Form opposites to these list words by adding 'un', 'ir', or 'in' to the beginning of each.

common	regular
conscious	capable

(b) Find list words which have the opposite meaning.

tame	lengthy
dead	energetic
foolish	similar
easy	

Prices down, benefits up and reduced waiting periods. It's a hard act to follow!

From August 1st. we've reduced the rates on most of our hospital tables.

We've added an entirely new extras range of benefits for dental, optical, chiropractic and other real and practical health care needs.

We've added an entirely new $75 a day hospital table.

And we've done away with most waiting periods, if you enrol in July, August or September, so that you can enjoy these advantages right away.

Now's the time to get in on the act. Drop into your nearest Medibank office or your Medibank chemist and pick up our new easy to follow literature for more details, or talk your needs over with us.

In over 5000 Medibank offices and chemists throughout Australia, we help you to choose the cover you really need, and make it quick and easy to claim. **medibank**

MC47 367 77V

7 Spellcomp

Divide the class into two teams. One person is nominated from each team by the teacher. The teacher then calls out a word from the list, and the two have to compete to see who can write the word correctly on the blackboard faster. First to complete the word wins a point for his/her team. Two new competitors are then nominated by the teacher, and so the game continues.

8 Follow the clues

Use the following clues to help you track down list words.

(a) Has a backward 'lug' in the middle.

(b) Ends with an 'able'.

(c) Contains a 'car'.

(d) Has a 'red' finish.

(e) Has a backwards 'fit' in the middle.

(f) Has a 'rent' at the end.

(g) Has an 'arm' in its middle.

(h) Begins with a type of hat.

(i) Starts with a scrambled 'fire'.

(j) Ends with a backwards 'evil'.

BUSY	SIMPLE
EXCITING	EXCELLENT
HEALTHY	TERRIBLE
WEALTHY	SUITABLE
IMPORTANT	AMAZING
FAVOURITE	TRUTHFUL
THIRSTY	LUCKY
GENEROUS	SIMILAR
FREQUENT	DEFINITE
CRUEL	SUSPICIOUS

25 More Descriptive Words

1 Fill in

Choose the best list word to fit into each of the following sentences.

(a) He suffered from ....e headaches.

(b) The police arrested him because of his ....s behaviour.

(c) A hot day makes you ....

(d) He was .... enough to find ten dollars.

(e) After the ....y day, Mother was tired out.

(f) He is so .... he would give you the shirt off his back.

(g) Anyone who is .... to animals should be punished.

(h) Fruit salad and icecream are my .... sweets.

(i) If you are always .... , then people will trust you.

2 Opposites

Form opposites (or antonyms) from the following list words by adding 'un', 'dis' or 'in' to the word.

	WORD	ANTONYM
	suitable	unsuitable
(a)	lucky	....
(b)	similar	....
(c)	truthful	....
(d)	definite	....
(e)	exciting	....
(f)	frequent	....
(g)	important	....

3 More opposites

Find list words opposite in meaning to the following words.

(a) kind   (b) complicated

(c) poor   (d) ill

(e) mean

4 Alphabetical

Arrange these list words in the order in which they would appear in a dictionary.

favourite	exciting
busy	frequent
thirsty	suitable
excellent	definite
terrible	suspicious

5 Word families

Fill in the blanks in the following word family table. The first one is done for you.

	ADJECTIVE	ADVERB	NOUN
(a)	busy	busily	business
(b)	amazing	....	....
(c)	suspicious	....	....
(d)	simple	....	....
(e)	truthful	....	....
(f)	thirsty	....	....
(g)	important	....	....

6 Use the clues

Identify, and write down, the list words suggested by the following clues.

(a) Has a place where a ship docks in its middle.

(b) Has a place where a prisoner is kept in its middle.

(c) Has a girl's name, beginning with 'r' in it.

(d) Has 'us' in the middle.

(e) Has a 'rib' in the middle.

(f) Begins with a backwards 'fed'.

(g) Has 'us' near its beginning and at its end.

(h) The last letter of the alphabet is in its middle.

(i) Has 'our' in the middle.

(j) Has an 'imp' in it.

7 Secret code

Use the reverse alphabet code (Z=1, Y=2, X=3, W=4, etc.) to solve the following. Each coded word is from your list.

(a) 7, 19, 18, 9, 8, 7, 2

(b) 8, 18, 14, 11, 15, 22

(c) 21, 9, 22, 10, 6, 22, 13, 7

(d) 8, 6, 18, 7, 26, 25, 15, 22

(e) 24, 9, 6, 22, 15

(f) 19, 22, 26, 15, 7, 19, 2

8 Spell-a-word (variation)

(a) Divide the class into two teams, with each member of Team 1 taking his turn to ask a different member of Team 2 to spell a word taken from previous word lists.

(b) Team 2 then asks members of Team 1 to spell words from other lists.

(c) Total the points earned by each team to find the winner. Scores can be kept on the blackboard.

9 Join up

Write down the left-hand column and add the correct endings from the right-hand column to form your list words.

(a) truth	ar
(b) gener	able
(c) terr	ful
(d) suit	ite
(e) defin	ous
(f) simil	ible

BELOW	TOWARDS
BENEATH	UNTIL
AMONG	POSSIBLY
BECAUSE	WHETHER
BESIDE	SHOULD
ALTHOUGH	OUGHT
ACROSS	REALLY
THROUGH	QUITE
EXCEPT	RATHER
WITHOUT	THEREFORE

26 Sentence-Building Words

1 Choosing and using

Write out the passage choosing and using the words as you go. Here are the words.

possibly	quite
among	because
without	rather
although	across
until	really

And here's the passage:

_____ it was _____ late, the plaza below street-level was packed with people all walking to and fro _____ the pavements.

_____ they were all doing some last minute shopping _____ closing time _____ the next day was a holiday.

Dogs wandered _____ the shoppers eating sandwich scraps but looking as if they would much _____ be gnawing bones. _____ a doubt, however, both shoppers and dogs were _____ enjoying themselves.

2 Quite and Whether

(a) Change the order of letters in QUITE to get a word meaning 'absence of noise'.

(b) Drop an H and add an A to WHETHER to get a word that means 'climate'.

(c) Now write sentences to show you know the difference between QUITE and _ _ _ _ _ _, and WHETHER and _ _ _ _ _ _ _ _.

3 Words showing position

Given one word, find the other seven. To help you, here are the other seven words that will fit into the squares:

below	through
beneath	without
beside	towards
among	

4 Wavelength

Wave 1 contains the first letter of each of seven words from the list. Wave 2 contains their second letter, and so on. Notice that Waves 6–8 contain fewer letters as words come to an end.
Your Job: find the seven words!

ave

1.   a   a   a   b
     b   b   b   c

2.   e   e   e   m
     e   l   t   o

3.   n   c   s   i
     l   r   o

4.   a   e   h
     n   o   s

5.   u   d   o
     g   a   w

6.   t   u   s
     s   e

7.   g   h
     h

8.

5 Mix and match

Join up the following sentences correctly.

(a) The bridge is down and therefore

(b) She had to decide whether

(c) Everything seemed to be running smoothly except

(d) We decided not to go surfing until

(e) The car passengers knew they ought

(f) It did not rain although

(g) He thought he should

(h) It was rather

there were plenty of clouds around.

that one tyre was down.

post the letter.

difficult to stay calm.

the wind died down.

it was better to go to a party or watch TV.

to do up their seat belts.

the river cannot be crossed.

6 Mixup

The following words have been scrambled. Unscramble them to find eight words from the list.

hebaten	wotsdar
towuhit	abucees
gotulhah	disebe
rotghuh	yerall

7 Find the words

Hidden among the following letters are six words from the list. The words may run vertically, horizontally or diagonally, and letters may overlap.

The six hidden words are: WITHOUT, QUITE, OUGHT, AMONG, UNTIL, SHOULD. Copy down the grid of letters, and shade in the words as you find them.

a	w	b	u	a	t	g	n	u	s
i	m	i	n	e	o	t	d	o	l
g	n	b	t	d	c	u	q	i	h
u	q	i	i	h	w	i	g	h	q
t	u	o	l	s	o	n	s	h	u
q	i	n	s	h	o	u	l	d	t
a	w	b	i	m	o	q	t	g	e
d	h	n	a	m	p	l	o	l	n

8 Homophones

Homophones are words with the same pronunciation but different meanings (from the Greek words *homoios*, 'same' and *phone*, 'sound'). For example, 'through' is a homophone of 'threw'.

Find homophones to go with the words below, and use each one in a sentence to show that you understand how they differ in meaning.

(a) scent	(b) quay
(c) pain	(d) waste
(e) cereal	

27 SCHOOL DAYS

LESSON	BOARD
STUDENT	SUBJECT
CLASS	RIGHT
FAILURE	WRITE
CHALK	WRONG
OFFICE	PENCIL
ESTIMATE	CORRECT
PAPER	STAFF
MESSAGE	MATHEMATICS
RUBBER	SCIENCE

1 Doubles

Write down all the words with double letters.

2 Jumbled meanings

Write the words in the left-hand column, and then match them with the correct meaning in the other column.

(a)	student	not a success
(b)	message	used to write on a blackboard
(c)	right	eraser
(d)	pencil	one who studies
(e)	rubber	used for wrapping up parcels
(f)	paper	a communication between people
(g)	failure	correct
(h)	chalk	usually made of wood and lead

3 Homophones

RIGHT and WRITE sound the same but their meanings are very different. Write the following, using the correct word.

(a) The pupils were asked to .... a composition about themselves.

(b) Do you have the .... answer?

Now do the same with LESSON and LESSEN.

(c) Antibiotics .... the side effects of a cold.

(d) The students found their spelling .... very interesting.

Now try BOARD and BORED.

(e) The pupils were .... when sport was cancelled because of the rain.

(f) A classroom looks tidier if the .... is cleaned after each lesson.

4 Crossword

The letters given should help you to complete the crossword puzzle with words from your list.

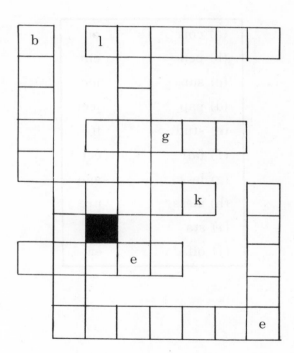

5 Match

Write down the left-hand column. Then make up a word from your list by attaching an ending from the right-hand column.

(a) corr	on
(b) pen	ent
(c) sub	ice
(d) pap	ject
(e) stud	ff
(f) fail	ect
(g) less	age
(h) mess	ure
(i) sta	cil
(j) off	er

6 Blanks

Fill in the missing letters.

(a) _ _ _ ff

(b) _ _ o _ _

(c) _ _ u _ e _ _

(d) _ e _ _ i _

(e) _ h _ l _

(f) _ c _ _ _ c _

(g) _ _ g _ _

(h) e _ _ i _ a _ e

7 Form bigger words

Fill in the blanks to make bigger words based on the words from the list.

(a) writ _ _ g	(b) class _ s
(c) offic _ _ l	(d) estimat _ _ n
(e) correct _ _ _	(f) scientif _ _
(g) message _	

8 Code

a	b	c	d	e	f	g	h	i	j	k	l	m	n	o	p	q	r	s	t	u	v	w	x	y	z
n	o	p	q	r	s	t	u	v	w	x	y	z	a	b	c	d	e	f	g	h	i	j	k	l	m

Each letter in the top row can be coded by using
the letter underneath it; e.g. j=w, p=c.

(a) e v t u g   (b) z n g u r z n g v p f

(c) o b n e q   (d) p u n y x

(e) f p v r a p r   (f) r f g v z n g r

(g) e h o o r e   (h) b s s v p r

(i) y r f f b a   (j) f h o w r p g

AVENUE CIRCUS

COLLEGE MARINA

FACTORY CONCERT

RESTAURANT COURTHOUSE

CINEMA HOTEL

ISLAND RESERVE

CATHEDRAL HOSPITAL

LIBRARY GARAGE

MUSEUM CARNIVAL

DISTRICT RESORT

28 Going Places

1 Dash it

Fill in the spaces with words from the list.

(a) The _____ where some of the _____ performers ate was next to the local lending _____.

(b) The skeletons of extinct animals were housed in the _____ which was built between the well-equipped _____ on one side and the _____ with the stained glass windows on the other.

(c) The _____ that manufactured window frames was to be found in an industrial _____. Trucks were loaded with window frames in an _____ at the back.

(d) The _____ employees ate lunch in a nearby grassy _____.

2 Circle

Five words from the list have been well and truly mixed within the circle. However, the letters that begin and end the words are shown outside the circle. Find the five words, making sure you use up all the letters as you do so.

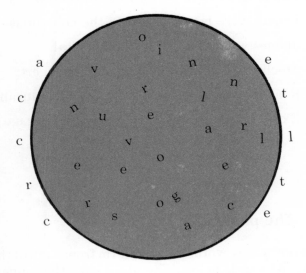

3 Places of relaxation and entertainment

Here are seven words from the list.

cinema   hotel
circus   resort
concert   restaurant
carnival

Try fitting them into the crossword. 'Restaurant' will start you off.

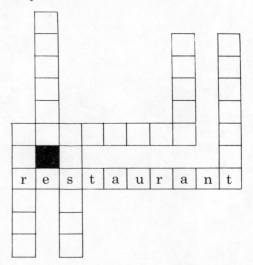

4 Place the people

Things are a little mixed in the following sentences. Clear them up by rewriting the sentences and putting the things that go together in their right places. You may have to change a letter here and there in your rewriting.

(a) Patients were being treated in the museum.

(b) Pop singers were performing in the library.

(c) Diners were being served in the courthouse.

(d) Judges were at work in the hospital.

(e) Mechanics were tinkering at the concert.

(f) Readers were making notes in the restaurant.

(g) Exhibits were being prepared in the garage.

5 The place race

See how many words you can form from each of the four list words below. The place with the longest tally wins!

| museum | marina | island | resort |

6 The R's have it!

Fill in words from the list around the letter 'r'.

(a) _ _ _ _ _ r _   (b) _ _ _ _ _ r _ _ _

(c) _ _ _ _ _ r _   (d) _ _ r _ _ _

(e) _ _ r _ _ _   (f) _ _ _ r _ _ _ _ _ _

(g) _ _ _ _ _ _ r _ _   (h) r _ _ _ _ _ _

(i) _ _ _ r _ r _   (j) r _ _ _ _ _ r _ _ _

(k) r _ _ _ r _ _   (l) _ _ r _ _ _

(m) _ _ r _ _ _ _ _

7 Education centre

Three places in the list are particularly linked with education. See if you can fit them in, given one letter for each word.

```
O        O
O        O
O        O
O        O               O
e   d   u   c   a   t   i   o   n
O        O               O
O                        O
                         O
                         O
                         O
                         O
```

8 Going together

Certain familiar words and phrases are often found together. Below, there are some such words and phrases. See if you can supply the words (from the list) that they're often found together with.

(a) three-star _ _ _ _ _ _

(b) shoe _ _ _ _ _ _ _ _

(c) tree-lined _ _ _ _ _ _ _

(d) _ _ _ _ _ _ _ of natural sciences

(e) holiday _ _ _ _ _ _ _

(f) nature _ _ _ _ _ _ _ _

(g) _ _ _ _ _ _ big top

(h) public _ _ _ _ _ _ _ _

(i) _ _ _ _ _ _ _ _ out-patients

(j) _ _ _ _ _ _ _ of advanced education

(k) pop _ _ _ _ _ _ _

(l) _ _ _ _ _ _ _ _ ambulance

BALLOON	SMILING
CHRISTMAS	ENTERTAIN
BIRTHDAY	REPLY
INVITE	PARCEL
PRESENT	AMUSE
SURPRISE	NOISE
WINNER	LAUGHTER
WELCOME	DEPART
CELEBRATE	GREETING
PRIZE	DELICIOUS

29 Parties

1 Front and back

Write down the words in the left-hand column and choose the correct ending from the right-hand column.

(a)	birth	come
(b)	sur	oon
(c)	wel	cel
(d)	Christ	vite
(e)	par	part
(f)	de	prise
(g)	in	mas
(h)	ball	day

2 Nouns

Form nouns from the following words.

(a) invite	(b) celebrate
(c) entertain	(d) amuse
(e) departs	

3 Find the words

Hidden in the following table are eight of your list words. They occur in a *straight* line (horizontally, vertically or diagonally) and some may read back to front. Copy the grid and shade the list words.

s	m	i	l	i	n	g	r
b	u	d	e	p	a	r	t
p	a	r	c	e	l	n	p
r	a	n	p	b	h	d	a
i	n	o	f	r	g	l	m
z	w	i	s	m	i	k	u
e	i	s	c	j	e	s	s
l	w	e	l	c	o	m	e

4 Revision of rules for adding ING

- When a word ends in a silent 'e', drop the 'e' before adding ING. Example: come—coming, make—making.
- When a word has a short vowel with only one consonant at the end, double the final consonant before adding ING. Example: stop—stopping, swim—swimming.
- When a word ends in two consonants, do not double the last letter when adding ING. Example: jump—jumping, work—working.

Now add ING to the following words.

LIST WORDS

(a) invite	(b) celebrate
(c) laugh	(d) present
(e) surprise	(f) win

PRACTICE WORDS

(g) welcome	(h) entertain
(i) smile	(j) greet
(k) amuse	(l) depart

5 Build up

Here is an example of word building in action.

amuse	
amus___	amuses
amus___	amused
amus_____	amusing
amus_____	amusement

Build up these words.

(a) depart
    depart_
    depart___
    depart____
    depart____

(b) invite
    invit___
    invit___
    invit____
    invit_____

(c) entertain
    entertain_
    entertain___
    entertain____
    entertain_____

6 Meanings

Select words from the list that mean:

(a) delightful to the taste

(b) to leave

(c) catch off guard or astonish

(d) package

(e) to ask courteously

(f) gladly received

(g) answer

(h) amuse

7 Blanks

Make new words based on the following list words by filling in the blanks.

(a) surprise   surpris_ _

(b) celebrate   celebrat_ _ _

(c) reply   repl_ _s

(d) noise   nois_

(e) welcome   welcom_ _

(f) present   present_ _

(g) laughter   laugh_ _

MEMBER	COUNCIL
MINISTER	CAPITAL
PREMIER	MAJORITY
QUEEN	DEBATE
ELECT	STATE
VOTER	NATION
GOVERN	FEDERAL
SENATE	MAYOR
LOCAL	MAGISTRATE
JUDGE	OFFICER

30 Government and Parliament

1 Word endings

Draw up the word houses below in your workbook.

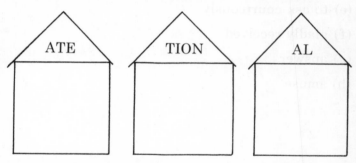

(a) Four words from your list end in ATE. Write them into your ATE house and think of another five words of your own ending in ATE to add to the house.

(b) Write the list word that ends in TION into the TION house, and add another five words with the same ending.

(c) Find the three list words ending in AL and copy them into the AL house. Add another five words which also end with AL.

2 Reform

Use the correct form of the list words to complete each of the following sentences.

(a) The choice of a .... was a popular one. [govern]

(b) Every three years a fresh .... must be held. [elect]

(c) The people were left to form their own .... about the performance. [judge]

(d) The leaders .... the issue until they reached a decision. [debate]

(e) People of every different .... were present at the opening of the Games. [nation]

3 Got the clues?

Use the following clues to help you identify list words.

(a) Rhymes with 'sinister'.

(b) Ends with the shortened form of the name 'Ernest'.

(c) Ends with the name 'Roy' spelt backwards.

(d) Has 'ice' in its middle.

(e) Has a start that is almost 'magic'.

(f) Has the word 'or' in the middle.

(g) Has 'me' forwards and backwards in it.

(h) Starts with a backwards 'bed'.

(i) Has a 'pit' in the middle.

(j) Rhymes with 'seen'.

4 Join up

Put the correct pieces of each word from Columns 1, 2 and 3 together, and so form seven words from the list.

	1	2	3
(a)	cap	ist	al
(b)	fed	ist	ity
(c)	mag	it	er
(d)	off	or	er
(e)	pre	er	rate
(f)	maj	mi	al
(g)	min	ic	er

5 Occupation

Find the list word which fits the person described by each statement in the work column below. The first one is done for you.

PERSON (list word)	WORK
(a) queen	the royal leader of a nation
(b)	the leader of a state government
(c)	casts a vote for whom he/she wants in the government
(d)	one of the two houses in the federal parliament
(e)	the leader of the local government in a town or city
(f)	a member of the government who is in charge of a particular sphere of work
(g)	person who is responsible for making decisions in legal matters

6 Alphabetical

Rearrange these words into the order in which they would appear in the dictionary.

mayor	magistrate
debate	state
council	judge
federal	majority
capital	voter

7 Spell-a-word

Divide the class into pairs, and draw up score pads like the ones below.

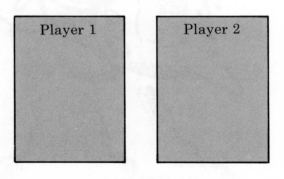

RULES

(1) Player 1 chooses a word from the list for his partner to spell. If it is spelt correctly, player 2 wins a point. If it is spelt incorrectly, player 1 wins a point.

(2) In his turn now, player 2 chooses another word from the list and asks player 1 to spell it. Scoring is the same.

(3) Note spelling errors as they occur. When all the words have been asked once, each player has one minute to review the words he has spelt incorrectly. After one minute he is required to spell each of these words to the partner, and then the partner spells all his earlier errors.

(4) In this latter section scoring is doubled. For every correct word, the speller receives two points. For every incorrect word his partner receives the two points.

(5) Total the points to find the winner.

QUEEN ELIZABETH SCHOOL
INDIVIDUAL RESOURCES

8 Forming new words

Look at the words in the left-hand column. Then fill in the blanks in the words opposite to form new words.

(a) state   statem<u>en</u>t

(b) elect   elect__o__

(c) judge   judgem<u>e</u>nt

(d) officer   offic<u>i</u>a<u>l</u>

(e) local   local__t__

(f) nation   nationa__i__y

(g) federal   federat<u>io</u>n

(h) council   councill<u>e</u>r

(i) senate   senato__

(j) govern   governo<u>r</u>

Index

The numerals refer to units, not pages.

large 22
laughter 29
laundry 14
leave 1
length 22
lens 10
lesson 27
library 28
lightning 6
listen 3
litre 22
little 22
loaf 16
local 30
lounge 14
lucky 25

magistrate 30
majority 30
manage 4
manager 8
margarine 16
margin 15
marina 28
mathematics 27
mayor 30
measure 20
member 30
memory 2
mention 3
message 27
method 4
microscope 10
middle 21
million 23
minister 30

mirror 13
moist 5
mother 17
motorist 11
mouth 5
multiply 23
museum 28

narrow 22
nation 30
neighbour 17
neither 23
nervous 12
noise 29
nothing 23
notice 10
nylon 20

observe 10
occasional 6
office 27
officer 11, 30
only 18
opening 9
opinion 2
order 3
ordinary 24
organize 4
ought 26
oval 9
oven 19
overcast 6

package 8
pair 20, 23
pants 20

paper 27
paragraph 15
parcel 29
parent 17
pass 9
passenger 11
patrol 7
pedal 13
penalty 9
pencil 27
perform 1
perfume 5
photograph 15
picture 14
piece 8
pillow 14
pilot 11
pleasure 7
pocket 20
polisher 19
possibly 26
powerful 24
praise 3
preface 15
premier 30
prepare 4
present 29
price 8
printer 15
private 17
prize 29
promise 3
publisher 15

quarrel 3
quarter 23

queen 30
question 3
quickly 18
quietly 18
quite 26

racing 13
radiator 19
raise 1
rarely 18
rather 26
reach 1
realize 2
really 26
reason 2
recognize 10
recorder 19
reduce 22
reference 15
reflector 13
refuse 3
regard 10
register 8
regular 24
relation 17
remain 1
remove 1
repair 4
reply 29
report 6
request 3
rescue 7
reserve 28
resort 28
restaurant 28
return 1

right 27
roast 16
rough 5
round 21
rubber 27

sandals 20
sandwich 16
satisfied 12
sauce 16
sausage 16
scarce 24
scent 5
science 27
score 9
scream 5
search 10
season 9
selected 9
selfish 12
senate 30
sensible 24
sentence 15
serious 12
serve 9
several 23
sewing machine 19
shelves 8
shining 13
shirt 20
shoes 20
shore 7
should 26
shower 6
sight 10
silent 5